COMBAT IN THE SKY

Books by ARCH WHITEHOUSE

Fiction

COMBAT IN THE SKY
BOMBERS IN THE SKY
FIGHTERS IN THE SKY
WINGS OF ADVENTURE
CRIME ON A CONVOY CARRIER

Nonfiction

TANK: EPIC HISTORY OF ARMORED WARFARE
THE YEARS OF THE WARBIRDS
THE YEARS OF THE SKY KINGS
HELL IN HELMETS
POOR BLOODY OBSERVERS
THE REAL BOOK ABOUT AIRPLANES

Combat in the Sky

by

ARCH WHITEHOUSE

DUELL, SLOAN AND PEARCE

New York

First edition

MANUFACTURED IN THE UNITED STATES OF AMERICA

VAN REES PRESS • NEW YORK

The author wishes to thank the following for permission to reprint: *The Saturday Evening Post:* "Offensive Sweep," copyright, 1942, by the Curtis Publishing Company; *Maclean's Magazine:* "Pip, Squeak and Wilfred" and "Seven Must Return"; *Blue Book:* "High in That Sunlit Silence," "Torpedo Attack," "Night Fighter," "Merton of the Mustangs," "What You Do at Twenty-two," "Bataan Landing," and "Assignment to Korea."

To

JAMES WARNER BELLAH

In Appreciation of Many Days and
Nights of Friendship

Author's Note

THIS is the third volume of my war-air stories. The previous selections were devoted to battle-mission adventures experienced by fighter pilots and bomber crews. In this presentation other representatives of war in the air make up the bulk of the tales. It will be noted that while the aircraft and missions are more varied, the characters behave much the same. We have gallant heroes and men of faint heart. There are dedicated men and playboys, gentlemen and roughnecks, but, as usual, the tune is piped to the courage or cowardice of men I may or may not have known.

Military aviators do not always behave as heroes in the classical sense. Only a mere handful are officially recognized for their heroic deeds, and those honored with the Congressional Medal of Honor or the Victoria Cross are seldom typical of the breed.

For years I have been trying to define human courage, or that intangible quality called bravery. I have seen many examples of military valor and have known dozens of men who have been awarded one or the other of the above premier decorations. I have plodded through many kinds of war activity and, with my comrades, have been despondent in defeat or vociferous in victory; but to this day I am unable to draw a line between what is accepted as courage and what is animal instinct. I cannot define cowardice, because I am fettered with what some publishers term my inherent sense of drama. In other words, the exploit is more impressive to me than the physical act that created it.

Many of us who have been honored with military decorations awarded in the field will, if honest, have considerable difficulty in outlining the action. We may be able to recite from memory the

stilted phraseology of the citation; but those words were penned
by men assigned to interpret the battle report and apply them to
the actions of the recipient. Usually, they fall far short of the
mark and seldom present the actual facts, the feelings, or hollow
dread that prevailed during the exploit.

If we present a decoration to an airman because he was so
devoted to duty that he destroyed a number of enemy aircraft,
for what are we rewarding him? From my personal observations,
most high-ranking aces of both world wars went through these
battles in the skies actually enjoying their experiences. They were
physically attuned to this type of action; but let us put these air
heroes in an armored tank or aboard a submarine—or in an infantry
foxhole—and note what their reactions will be under these unfamiliar circumstances.

I present my own case. I was of doubtful value as a ground
soldier, but on transferring to the flying service—then widely
considered a suicide club—I was unaccountably content and confident during all types of air action. Whatever success I had, or
how I behaved under these varied circumstances, had little to do
with any voluntary action on my part: I enjoyed flying on the
old Western Front. Mature consideration several years later con-
vinced me that heroism in military action is a very uncertain
quality.

I have selected several types of lead characters in the stories in
this book, but whether they are heroes in the conventional sense
is a matter to be debated. They are men I have met or been told
of who actually behaved as do the central figures in these tales.

I knew a man who acted as did Tommy Dobbs in "Offensive
Sweep." There were half-a-dozen Old Jacksons who wore "Pip,
Squeak, and Wilfred" ribbons. They told me many of the stories
I wrote. I still remember Chauncey Boyne of "High in That
Sunlit Silence." I met him one night in a Norfolk pub called The
White Hart, and he told me about his old man, who in turn gave
me the idea for the original story title—"Medal Bloke"—only

someone showed me a copy of John Magee, Jr's, sonnet, "High Flight," and I couldn't resist that memorable line.

You wouldn't call Merton Updyke Glassford in "Merton of the Mustangs" a hero, but there will always be a few Mertons in any war and they will always be guided to glory by something as ridiculous as Fat Anna. Our heroes are not always commissioned officers. Look at Corporal Pete Coyne, who believed all he read in the old pulp magazines and because of that questionable morale blundered his way to glory in "Bataan Landing." The hoary policy of teamwork gets a raking over in "Seven Must Return," and "What You Do at Twenty-two" will, I hope, bring nostalgic pleasure to many who lived their war at that memorable bracket of their time.

They are all offered as fictional characters in these pages, but each and every one had a serial number in some outfit somewhere. They were among my friends, and knowing them has long soothed the loneliness of the writer's cubicle. I hope the reader will enjoy meeting them half as much as I enjoyed penning their adventures and exploits.

ARCH WHITEHOUSE

Livingston, New Jersey

Contents

COMBAT IN THE SKY

Offensive Sweep

Every wartime airman secretly nurtures his own special brand of fear or tastes the canker of some particular doubt. It may be the dread of fog, or fire. He may tremble at the thought of a mid-air collision; he may awake at night, streaming with sweat, and chop off the nightmare of a jammed cockpit hatch. Some fear coming in with their wheels up; others believe they'll get it one night from an ack-ack shell intended for a Jerry raider.

Flight Lieutenant Tommy Dobbs was one of those haunted specimens of the RAF. The psychologists might decide that Tommy suffered the thrashings of a dual personality. I wouldn't know about that. I was simply his Air Intelligence officer at the time and I pieced together most of this from snatches dropped here and there by Wing Commander Osgood. Of course old Osgood can tell a fine tale when he has a mind, and I've never been quite certain where his facts ended and his fiction began.

Tommy was the best Hurricane pilot in Number 131, and we all knew it. He used to say he ought to be because his father had been the best damned Camel pilot on the Somme in the other war. We never checked on that, but old Osgood said he remembered his father, and we let it go. But as I say, you can't tell where Osgood's yarns skip over the points of fact and glide along the high iron of fiction.

Tommy Dobbs was almost too tall for Hurricanes—most of his height was in his long lancer legs. He'd been turned out in the perfect mold for RAF dress kit. He was fair, with a nice set of yellow teeth that complimented nature's studied irregularity, his

3

eyes were the color of tawny port, and he had the voice of a genteel Latin professor.

The Hurricanes of Number 131 had been revitalized for low-level sweeps into occupied areas across the Channel. The Hurries had been transformed from deadly altitude fighters into attack machines that raked and battered enemy ground targets with air cannon.

Number 131 was slamming out of Hawksley and was giving the coastal recognition signal before plunging across the Ditch for Marquise. Dobbs was leading Green flight and Squadron Leader Bootles was up front with White. Bootles was one of those theatrically handsome devils who managed to blot out the glories of a godlike profile with a scraggy mustache that hung like the dreary fringe of a damp dugout curtain.

"Poleax Squadron clear! Calling Southdown control. Calling Southdown control. Over to you, Southdown," Squadron Leader Bootles reported. "Any business, Southdown?"

The duty officer at Hawksley accepted the code call and responded, "Southdown calling Poleax Squadron. Maintain operation plan. Twenty-plus F.-W.'s patrolling at eighteen thousand north of Calais. Ignore!"

"Thank you. Poleax Squadron will continue operation plan," Bootles answered.

"Maintain operation plan," Dobbs repeated to himself with bitterness. "Why can't we intercept? No, we have to do offensive sweeps." He twisted in his seat and drew back a ventilation panel and stared down at the lightship blinking a clearance signal. He clamped his jaw tighter and looked back farther.

"He's looking back again," Pinky Lyman muttered. "There's a man with a streak, if I ever saw one."

For two weeks now Pinky had caught his flight commander looking back. Pinky knew, and Topper Hurrell, off the other elevator, knew—Dobbs was going to chuck it again the first chance he got.

Tommy Dobbs squirmed in his seat and thumbed the bind of his parachute straps. What good was a parachute on low-altitude sweeps? What chance had a man at this height? He fumed to himself. "We could nail half a dozen of those F.-W.'s."

They were across now and getting the opening blasts from the flak ships. They dithered through the billowing surf of concussion and Bootles opened the formation for safety. Dobbs moved over and his flight sideslipped with him.

The main road from Marquise to Guines was racing along below them when something tonked with a metallic clang behind Dobbs' head. His antenna pylon flopped over and began to beat the side of the Hurricane with frenzied lashes. Tommy tried to twist around farther to inspect the details of the damage, and his eyes met those of Lyman. He could see Pinky cupping his flap mike over, but caught only a slight murmur in his earphones.

"Nothing doing!" he growled, and gave the washout signal to Pinky through the hatch window. He went on building up his case to himself. "You take over, Pinky. My set's dead!"

Lyman could hear nothing from Dobbs, but sensed what his flight commander meant when he swung over and dropped back. Pinky moved up, reported through to the skipper, and Dobbs took over the outside corner of the formation. He glanced over toward Hurrell who was trying to figure out the damage. The antenna pylon was still beating the flanks of the Hurricane, and Dobbs could see the coppery wound of a stripped lead and he wondered how long it would hold.

The Hurries were clear of the shore flak now and Bootles was taking them down for the sweep. A new constriction of anxiety clutched at Tommy—all he could get now was the carrier hum through his earphones. He saw Red, White, and Yellow flights swinging into a line-astern formation, preparing for their attack on the freight barges in the canal north of Watten. Hurrell was sitting erect and tense, and Pinky S-turned a minute and fell in behind Whately of Yellow Flight.

Dobbs saw his chance and waved to Hurrell, sending him to a

place behind Pinky, and then tagged on to the end of the line. Up front Bootles was already getting the first dish of defense flak.

"I don't know what I can do with a dead set. I'm not a mind reader." Tommy argued with himself as he twisted and stared back again. The Hurries were so low now that the fawn-colored coast line was out of sight. What about those F.-W.'s? They'd be the only bluebirds over the white cliffs of Dover.

Red flight was already thumping down at the brownish blobs in the canal. Bootles' face fringe would be sticking out like spines on a catfish. When he got back he'd bellow about the sweep all the way from the dispersal bays to the Operations office.

The thoughts of all that made Tommy swing over and begin to climb toward the west. "A man doesn't have a chance that low," he consoled himself.

The lone Hurricane raced for the coast and Tommy breathed normally again once the blue of the strait could be seen below and behind his trailing edge. He drew back his greenhouse top, set the reflector sight for a four-engine wing span, and sought the Focke-Wulf bombers. Instead of drumming up his fear, the flailing antenna pylon only urged him on. Now all the tension was off. He was back where he belonged, back where he had won his D.F.C. in this mad cocking main where Hurricane and Spitfire had driven off the aerial invaders. This was the battlefield he knew and enjoyed, where he had sent seventeen enemy planes to their doom.

He caught the first F.-W. over Lydd as it was struggling back with one inboard engine dragging a sooty streamer. He identified her carefully on her large square fin—there must be no mistaking her.

Tommy Dobbs whanged over and watched her pass, and then sought his point on the long tubular bomb chamber. This was lone-wolf stuff over the home grounds and he gloried in it. His fingers slipped the safety ring off the gun button and he moved in up-sun, and charged savagely at the wavering Focke-Wulf

Kurier. The pinkish gleam of the sight appeared on the reflector glass and he treadled his nose into position.

"A sitter, and a wounded sitter, at that," he grumbled, "but she'll do."

He watched the evasive action of the Kurier's tail controls as he moved in close and fitted her wing span inside the ring of the glowing sight. The big bomber tried to escape on what was left of three engines, but Tommy was over Kent and there was no fear in his heart.

"They can have their offensive sweeps. Nothing much to show for it when you're through, and you stand a chance of . . ."

The big F.-W. Kurier was dead on and Tommy pressed the button. Four bull-throated guns chugged a five-second burst, and chunks of dural danced excitedly from the Kurier's trailing-edge flaps. He rammed in harder, pressed again, and then swung up as he cleared the tabbed rudder by inches.

The flailing antenna pylon beat a deprecatory tattoo on the fuselage as Tommy came over and sought the harassed F.-W. again. A Knott-Bremse gun snapped its venom across the sky and stitched a zigzagged selvage along the edge of his port aileron. The stick trembled with the drag of the perforations and Tommy's lips drew back until the pink of his gums went white. He tried her gently, sideslipping away. The aileron answered, but whistled in derision with the thumping of the fractured pylon.

Then he went action mad. The Hurricane was horsed around again and he punched her for the angle between the starboard wing root and the fuselage. His guns exploded in chorus again and the smoke-scarfed motor threw its antlered head back and ripped itself clear of the bearers. There was a spate of splintered flame, a gush of waxy smoke, and the inboard motor rolled drunkenly across the wing and slithered off into space.

"That's worth all the sweeps we'll ever complete." But the thrill of victory was subdued by the realization that he had deserted his flight. "They can't say I haven't earned my keep today."

He watched the doomed F.-W. begin its spin down toward
Romney March. The free wing fluttered off like a broken
butter paddle and rinsed the sky with iridescent spray from
slashed fuel containers. Two figures, all arms and legs, suddenly appeared beneath scallop-edged canopies of *ersatz* silk.

"Go on down," Tommy muttered, as his mind bridged a
quarter of a century of morbid reflection. "They'll soon have
you behind the wire. There you'll stay, eating your hearts out
for freedom and a chance to take ten full strides in any direction.
They'll coop you up until you scream and wish you'd never
pulled that rip cord."

Dobbs circled the airdrome twice while the control lorry
snapped its invitation to come in. On the far side, the Hurricanes
of Number 78 Squadron were crawling out of their dispersal
bays and picking their beetlelike way through the linkage
of bomb dollies.

He waited, and circled again in the hope that Bootles and the
rest would return and give him the opportunity to check in with
them. However, the green Aldis light was insistent, and he had to
go in alone.

There was the usual grouping of administrative authority outside the Operations hut when he went up to book in. Wing Commander Osgood and his adjutant, a caliper-shaped lad who walked
with a heavy cane, saw Dobbs approaching. Tommy caught the
twist of Osgood's mouth and sensed that he was in for it when
they strode off toward the hut without waiting for him.

"They've got nothing on me," Dobbs protested for his own
satisfaction as he attempted to light a cigarette with nonchalance
"I brought back enough lace to satisfy anyone. I'll need a whole
new wing panel."

Inside the hut there was a tense, sultry decompression-chamber
touch to the room. Osgood was scowling at a Signals flimsy which
had just been handed to him by a WAAF sergeant. The adjutant
was listening silently at a telephone and rearranging a list of

names on the Pilots Available board behind his desk. He turned suddenly and pointed an accusing finger at Dobbs. "You! You're next, Dobbs!"

Tommy tried to interpret that as the wing commander shoved the flimsy back at the girl. "Tell him not to worry about Dobbs. Dobbs is back. I want a full confirmation on Hurrell."

"Hurrell?" Tommy inquired. "What happened to Hurrell?"

The adjutant lad broke in. "That puts you next, Dobbs. Ten days, beginning tonight. Hurrell won't be back. You move up one."

None of it made sense to Tommy. He fumbled with a patrol-report form as he studied first the wing commander and then the pasty face of the war-shattered adjutant. The trial was opening and the jury was being selected. The cleaver was being honed for the legal ration. The girl waited a few seconds, holding the door open. Tommy could hear the teletypes clacking in derision and the voice of a corporal clerk telling someone to get off the line and not obstruct the war.

"That's all! Shove off!" Osgood snapped officiously at the girl.

"Yes, sir. I'll report Flight Lieutenant Dobbs in."

"And have his leave warrant made up," the adjutant added.

The wing commander listened as though he were trying to finish a jigsaw puzzle by mental telepathy.

"Cleared off at the right time, eh, Dobbs?" The adjutant was sorting some papers.

"No, I—that is—" Then it all enveloped him and pinioned his arms down to his sides.

"What happened to you, Dobbs?" the wing commander added.

"I was out of communication, sir. Chunk of flak took out my antenna pylon. I couldn't contact Bootles."

"What happened to Hurrell?" Osgood persisted.

"He was on Pinky's tail when I cleared off. Last man, like."

"Up to then you were the last man?"

The scene came back to Tommy and was highlighted in his mind against a contrasting mat of his own black reflections.

Hurrell went in behind Pinky, believing Dobbs was tailing him. If a Jerry coursed in from somewhere behind, Hurrell would never know it.

"You see, I couldn't let them know I was clearing off. I felt that being out of touch, I'd be something of a—"

From a half-squatting position above his office chair Osgood broke in with, "Then you didn't tackle the barges?"

"No, sir. I cleared off, crossed the Ditch on my own, and had a scramble with a Focke-Wulf. I piled her up in Romney Marsh."

He might just as well have said, "My batman didn't polish my buttons this morning, sir," for all the effect the statement had on Osgood. The wing commander's razor-annealed chin was jutting out like the front gun turret of a Lancaster.

"I don't suppose it occurs to you, Dobbs, that Hurrell . . ." the wing commander began, but his sense of fairness interposed. He leaned over, snapped the interdepartmental phone switch, and said, "See if you can get a confirmation on a Focke-Wulf down in Romney Marsh." He turned to the adjutant and added, "Go out and see if you can trace that, Saunders."

"If Dobbs says he got one," the adjutant pronounced as he went out, "you can bet he got it. Good hunting, Dobbs!"

The wing commander watched the door close, shoved his cap back, and dabbed his forehead with a massive colored handkerchief. Dobbs studied him and realized for the first time that Osgood wore ribbons under his wings that testified to his service in the other war.

"Sit down, Dobbs." Osgood pointed to a chair with the stem of his pipe. "You know," he began, "it isn't half as bad as it seems."

"Well, I am a bit worried about it, sir, now that Hurrell has packed up. I was afraid you'd think . . ."

"No, not that. I mean being a prisoner of war. They had me for a while in the last show."

Tommy stiffened but didn't rise to it.

"I managed to get away, though." The wing commander leaned back and blew a long blue plume toward the ceiling. "You can still carry on, even though they have you behind the wire. As a matter of fact, it's your duty."

"I don't quite understand, sir."

"I know why you're afraid to go across the Ditch," Osgood said bluntly. "You were a great pilot when we were knocking them down over the Estuary. You ought to be a squadron leader by now, but you're not. On offensive sweeps across the Channel, you're a proper washout. You'll use any excuse to clear off and come home."

Dobbs took the whiplashing without flinching. The fester had been lanced. The relief that his secret fear was shared and known took all the strain out of his shoulders. The throb left his temples and he relaxed for the first time since entering the Operations hut. He wondered how it would end. Probably ship him off to some Penguin Roost where he wouldn't have to fly or risk a forced landing in enemy territory.

It was all over now, and he was glad. There would be ten days of freedom in which he could gloat in God's warm sunshine. Ten days—two hundred and forty hours—of leisure and laughter, chesting the ribbon that tokened his service. He'd be whole and unmaimed when it was all over, and he'd be able to speak the language of the warriors and claim membership in the confraternity of fighting men at reunions and Empire Day celebrations. There was a home somewhere in the Cotswolds, a bit of ground he could call his own. He'd fought for it and done his best to settle the score, so long unpaid.

He felt he ought to tell the wing commander of that hopeless quest. It might explain it a bit. Perhaps Osgood would understand if he told that story.

Instead, the wing commander told one.

"I used to fear the same thing." Wing Commander Osgood offered his tobacco pouch and went on, "I quite understand the feeling, Dobbs. A patrol forty miles over in our day was practically asking for it. I went down during the Cambrai show."

"Didn't you go almost mad, sir?"

"Not at first. I was shocked and numb with the realization that I was through—that, for me, the war was over. I tried to argue with myself that it was engine trouble. That, whatever happened, I would come out alive and with all that belonged to me. I tried to believe that, but somehow the idea just didn't click. I felt that somehow I'd chucked it, and began to wonder if those I'd left behind would question. There used to be some nasty stories about chaps who were taken prisoner in those days."

"But you can't help engine trouble, sir."

"You can fake engine trouble."

"But how can you prove it? A man wouldn't set down deliberately in enemy territory, sir!"

"You don't have to prove it. You can only judge a man by the way he acts after he's put behind the wire."

Tommy wondered why the wing commander was telling him this. "Did you know anyone who actually chucked it that way, sir?"

"I knew one man who didn't," Osgood said after a repack of his pipe. "He was the gamest man I met in the last war. Should have had the V.C."

The icy chains were tightening up again and a slow shudder of intuition trickled across Tommy's shoulder muscles. "What were you going to say—about this other man, sir?"

Osgood folded his tobacco pouch with studied deliberation. "A small group of us wanted to clear ourselves, so to speak. This man organized us. He was a fighter if ever there was one. He drew up our plans and devised an ingenious arrangement for digging a tunnel. He made a pair of bellows out of a tennis-racket press. He worked out a compass with a piece of razor blade, and invented means of obtaining maps and supplies for a mass escape."

"Bellows, sir?"

"Of course. Before we were through our tunnel was nearly

thirty yards long and we had to devise ways of getting fresh air through to the man who happened to be working in it."

"It sounds incredible!"

"It was hard work, but it saved many of us from a state of depression that might have finished us. Eventually, after weeks of effort, we reached our point outside the wire."

Tommy listened in rapt fascination.

"That's where this chap comes into the story. Twenty-six of us made up the escape party. Someone had to be leader, and this chap assumed the post from the start. He decided to go first and make the final break-through of the tunnel. Touchy business, that."

"And you all got away?"

"Twenty-five of us did, with varying success. Only about four finally reached England safely. But it was this leader bloke who made it possible. Should have been awarded the V.C. for that show," the wing commander repeated reflectively.

"You mean his going out first?"

"He broke the tunnel through, crawled out, and then distracted the attention of the sentries and drew their fire, until he went down. That's how we got away. There was never any question about his intention. He was determined to get as many of us into the clear as possible. Being a prisoner made no difference—he never gave up."

Tommy Dobbs stood up. "That's the story you wanted to tell me, isn't it, sir?"

"I often wondered if you knew—since your name is Dobbs, too." The wing commander slowly tapped his teeth with his pipestem.

"All we got was a notice from the War Office saying he had died a prisoner of war. We always wondered about that." Tommy spaced his words reverently.

"I think you ought to know. None of us would tell it before. It seemed unfair to add that to a bit of paper from the War Office."

"You don't know Mother. She would have been very proud."

"You can tell her when you get home. You're leaving tonight?"

"No, sir! Will you take care of that? I'm letting Bootles go in my place." Tommy Dobbs was in charge now, and the wing commander knew it.

"Righto! I'll brief your lot at fifteen hours. We've got another show late this afternoon. Something to do with a sortie against enemy transport. It'll be a bit sticky, but it's in a worthy cause." The wing commander smiled.

"I'll shove off and put the scourge on my riggers. They'll have to replace a wing in record time. See that Bootles clears off, will you, sir?" and Tommy produced a rare smile.

Wing Commander Osgood briefed them at three fifteen. They were a pretty sour lot when they learned that they were to be led by Flight Lieutenant Dobbs. Still, Pinky Lyman would be on hand, and he could take over once Dobbs found an excuse to pull out and clear off home.

". . . Along the main line here between Bruges and Ostend," said the wing commander who stood beside a photograph enlarged and thrown on a roller screen, "you'll have a double target, as you all know. There's a lot of traffic on the railroad lines, and just as much in the canal that runs parallel with the metals."

"Any particular reason for this show, sir?" Sergeant Birchfield of White Flight inquired.

"Coming to that. We have reason to believe that Old Nasty is moving troops and coastal-defense supplies into the Ostend-Dunkirk area. He evidently believes we're going to try a commando raid or something there. Let him think what he will. We'll take advantage of the targets offered, if you get what I mean."

"Concentrate as much as possible on rolling stock—particularly their engines," the Intelligence group captain broke in. "We'd like to see a few boilers bashed about. They can't repair engine boilers in an afternoon."

The wing commander closed it with, "That's all. At Readiness from 16:30 hours. Any questions?"

They were all too tired to go into it any further. Tommy Dobbs watched them as they filed out. He knew they had one question but were too proud to present it. He wanted to stop them and tell them not to worry, but he knew there could be only one token of assurance, and he couldn't give it until they were well across the Ditch.

They took off shortly before five o'clock, burdened with the code designation, Parsnip Patrol—selected because the wing commander liked the vegetable.

"He really means he hopes we'll go so low down we'll come back with a mixed grill in our air scoops," Pinky Lyman belly-ached as they crossed to the dispersal bays.

"Good hunting, Parsnip Patrol. Your vector one-eight-four. One-eight-four. Angels four over South Foreland for crossing."

That gave Tommy his course and orders to cross the Ditch at four thousand feet. He grinned and cupped the flap mike over.

"Hello, Southdown control. Vector one-eight-four. Angels four. Receiving you strength seven. Over to you."

Pinky Lyman listened, and waited for Dobbs to give the order to climb. They were whanging over the Folkestone-Canterbury line at less than five hundred feet. Pinky glanced across at young Sparling who had come out of reserve to take Hurrell's place. Pinky's eyes said, "I told you he didn't give up that leave for nothing. This will be a juicy hop."

"Hello, Parsnip Patrol." Dobbs spoke over his set to the rest of the squadron. "We're maintaining a low level all the way across. You might as well get used to it now. Tighten up in flights of Vee."

"Have you been inoculated with the groveling germs of a mole?" Pinky inquired as he skillfully slipped his wing tip up closer to Dobbs' tail.

"Why bother with wings?" Mudder Maddox broke in from

the outside tip of Red Flight. "Just put the wheels down and
we can use the roads."

"His doctor says he should stay out of Ferris wheels and chapel
balconies. The rarefied air does something to him," Clinker
Jones added.

Dobbs listened but did not hear. His mind was on a quest of
glorious promise—a quest he had pledged himself to fulfill more
than twenty years before, but until Wing Commander Osgood
had primed the charge he had never been able to muster the
courage. A brash boyhood covenant had hung like a lodestone
in his breast for years.

"He was the first one out," he repeated to himself. "He hadn't
chucked it. He still continued to fight, even behind the wire."

He glanced around and sensed the responsibility he had assumed in flying up front. They were relying on him now. He
was the leader in this mad quest, and he was responsible that as
many as possible got back. He cupped his mike over again and
spoke "Parsnip Patrol, check! Attention, Parsnip Patrol. Are all
machines airworthy? Check by flights, please."

One by one they reported through—all were serviceable.
Pinky added, "The only thing I'm worrying about is that we'll
get stuck in a tank trap before we hit the coast. You just took the
froth off some old gaffer's beer in that pub yard back there."

Dobbs was laughing now. These were his pals and he knew
they were enjoying it. He'd show them he wasn't windy. He'd
take them on a sweep they'd long remember. What if they were
taken prisoner? You could always do something about it and
keep raising hell. Someone has to go first.

They rammed across the Ditch so low they left a shimmering
wake on the easy Channel rollers. Dobbs led them toward Dunkirk and then cut out northeast when a fleet of E-boats came
out to greet them.

"We'll take care of you on the way back," Tommy growled.
He gave his final order at Middelkerke and wished them luck.

"Attention, Parsnip Patrol. Line astern and pick up your targets from the marshaling yard outside Ostend. Take it all the way to Bruges and rendezvous over Oostcamp at three thousand."

"Best of luck, Skipper!" called Pinky.

"Thanks, Pinky. Tallyho!"

The cannon-fanged Hurricanes cleared the flak by the simple expedient of going in so low that the guns could not be depressed enough to get them.

Dobbs led the way down the Avenue de la Reine and with a scream of power turned over the Laiterie Gardens. He poked his nose sharply at the huddle of barges in the Bassins du Commerce and swept around to his right and slammed a long burst into the Maritime Station.

The rest followed him blindly, as though they were laced together with an invisible wire. Guns mounted on the sheds of the marine basin rattled bronze-tipped slugs through the metal wings and played a tympanic concerto along the fuselages.

"Send it up, Jerry!" Tommy cried. "You might as well waste it on us as anyone. Here's a packet for those oil barges."

His guns flamed and roared again, and he pulled out, turned tight, and thumped through the belches of shell concussion for the marshaling yards beyond the station. With a switchback hoik he swept over the hotel and poured short, stabbing bursts into the cluttered rail traffic.

There was a roar somewhere below him and a blazing Hurricane projectiled into a goods shed and disappeared. Tommy clamped his teeth and swore. He cleared the marshaling yard and plunged on along the tracks, peered up into his retrospect mirror and saw his madcaps were following him.

As an engine loomed around a bend and reached a stone bridge, Dobbs steeplechased over a set of semaphores and nosed down at it. His 20-mm. slugs drilled through the head plate, and a festoon of steam shot out and threw an eiderdown back over the cab. Tommy slashed through the vapor and plunked heavy-caliber stuff into the tarpaulins with short, jolting bursts that

flicked up metal, wood, and canvas. Behind him, Pinky was but-
toning down anything Dobbs' shells were perforating.

Another and another were met as they scorched along the
railway. From the sides, other Hurricanes were lancing in at
tight angles and hammering the loaded barges, or drilling the
boiler casings of the locomotives. Frantic flak exploded overhead
and drenched them with shrapnel and shell casing. Still, the
Hurricanes swept on until they reached the curve of the lines
that swung south into the Central Station at Bruges.

Dobbs glanced at his ammo indicator and saw he had conserved
enough for a final smash at the supply dumps heaped along the
Rampart du Béguinage. The goods were stacked high and were
well defended by ack-ack of varying sizes which coughed deep-
throated objections with graze fuses.

"When I think of all I've been missing." Tommy scowled as he
squinted into his reflector sight. "I could boot myself. Getting
old F.-W. sitters over the Estuary—and getting a D.F.C. for it,
mind you—when I could have been enjoying this. And I let
Bootles go on leave in my place because I thought he might be
worn out. Why, this is great! I'll bet Dad would have loved this."

He was on again, and the Hurricane roared down at the
stacked supplies that blocked in the narrow-gauge railway. His
guns responded to his touch and screamed their battle chorus.
The Hurricane recoiled against the impact of muzzle blast. The
quadruple streams of spinning metal bit in deep and torched the
inflammables. He put the flaming finger on Jerry's offensive material and the rest of the formation ganged up and rubbed it out.

They re-formed—with but two missing—over Oostcamp, and
raced for the Channel.

"Now take it easy, Skipper. You're well over five hundred feet,"
Pinky warned. "You'll catch cold."

Tommy Dobbs laughed hard, and it was the first time they'd
heard him really laugh since he had joined the squadron.

"A very nice show," Mudder Maddox offered when they were
in the clear. "Now, if only old Bootles would go in that way."

"You were really very nasty to them, Skipper." Pinky spoke over his set. "Where did you pick up such offensive manners?"

"I'll tell you about that someday. It's in the family," Tommy explained. "Close in, lads. Let's put on a show going home."

"He wants to put on a show going home!" Pinky wailed.

High in That Sunlit Silence

HIS name was Chauncey Boyne, and he was marked by the aristocratic stamp they use on a man whose forebears long made history in County Antrim. He was as slim and lithe as a steeplechase whip. There were times when he spoke like one. Chauncey had neat, compact shoulders—the kind designed expressly for evening clothes, or the mess jacket of the Eighth Hussars—his hands were those of an artist, and there was music vibrating all through him. It came out, not only in piano chords and melody, but in every move he made.

Most of the time the music had the cadence and swing of a military quickstep; full assurance that Chauncey was born to serve.

If you thrill to the dock-walloper type of Celt, Lieutenant Boyne is not your man. He proudly answered to his name of Chauncey, and it was well to use it with suitable dignity. Back at Charles Field they tell of a cadet who made the grim mistake of crying, "Oh, Chauncey!" just as an experiment. To this day that cadet believes he backed into a prop.

Chauncey Boyne took to flying as naturally as his ancestors had taken to hunters and timber toppers. His father, Major Conway Boyne, had been the finest horseman on the Curragh. His grandfather had won the Grand National back in 1907—or perhaps it was 1908—and after the family moved to Virginia, life went on much the same. They raced point to point, bred horseflesh for the show rings, drank bourbon instead of Bushmills, and made more money than they had thought was ever minted.

The Boynes stocked well and knew their job, and, better

still, employed the right people—experienced hands who spoke their dulcet tongue. So much like Portglenone did Virginia seem that it was not until 1939 that they realized it was a county in a foreign country. That was when Chauncey hacked into Roanoke and demanded to be accepted for the war. It took some time and several references to a wall map to convince him that Virginia was in no way mixed up in the conflict.

That night the Boynes held a council of war. The subject was the matter of a regiment for Chauncey. No Boyne in the past three hundred years had reached his majority without being commissioned in the King's Royal Eighth Hussars. Opposite the large fireplace, a glassed-in cabinet gleamed with Con Boyne's regimentals: the royal blue tunic with four rows of shining decorations; the busby, with its scarlet distinction bag; the drum cloth with the Harp and Crown insigne; the crossed sword-belt, a traditional regimental marking claimed since the battle of Saragossa in 1710.

"Can't imagine what we've been thinkin' all these years," the major muttered. "It'll be weeks before he can get into action at this rate. Ride he can, but the boy knows nothing about the saber or dismounted action."

Old Teigue Boyne, who had been a colonel in the Eighth and still limped from a shattered knee suffered in South Africa, added, "No matter. Get him in so he's eligible for the campaign medal." Old Teigue was a warped figure of a man close on eighty years of age; his face was a mass of browned wrinkles, the top of his bald head was suety white, and a wisp of gray hair tufted out over each ear. His speech was the rasping chirp of a cricket as he looked up with a sniff. "I suppose they still strike campaign medals, eh?"

Ellen Boyne, Chauncey's mother, sat pensive with her fine hands in her lap. "They'll niver give a ribbon as fine and gay as the African General Service," she said.

Major Boyne reached for the telephone while old Teigue

cackled. "Can't hold a match to the Khedive's Sudan medal of 1910."

"Get me the War Office." Conway Boyne spoke uncivilly to the operator. "What's that? ... No, I mean the British War Office. Don't you know there's a war on? The War Office in London, I tell ye."

"Same trouble I had in Roanoke," Chauncey explained. "The man in the office ..."

Old Teigue broke in. "Niver speak of a man. Ye always refer to him by his rank."

"It's not the same as you had it in the Eighth," Chauncey muttered, and went over to the regimental case and studied Con's ribbons.

"Practically everything a man can win there," Ellen Boyne said as she joined Chauncey.

"He didn't get the Victoria Cross," old Teigue cackled from across the room. "Took old Teigue to get that one. At the relief of Kimberley it was."

Con Boyne returned the telephone to its prongs and peered moodily at the case. "She said she'll call me back if she can get through. I presume Kilmayne is still at the War Office."

"Of course he is." Ellen added, "He's too old for anything else."

"How long did you serve to get all these, Father?" Chauncey asked respectfully.

"About four years," Major Boyne replied. "We fought at Givenchy, the Somme, Cambrai, Bapaume, Mons, Rosières, Amiens, Albert, and Beaurevoir. We weren't always mounted, mind ye," he added sadly. "They tried to make gravel-crushers of us, but when they wanted someone to chase von Hindenburg back to the Rhine, whom did they call on? The Dirty Eighth, son." Con Boyne clicked his heels. *Pristinae virtutis memores—* Mindful of former valour," he read from his old collar badge.

Ellen Boyne rolled the glass door back and ran her fingertips along the silken ribbons. "Aren't they beautiful?" she asked tenderly. "Come the day, son, ye'll have several rows, too. They're the mark of a man, and ye'll come home, and ye'll make a fine husband, and ye'll have a fine family to take care o' ye tunics, and see to it ye medals are properly mounted according to the order of precedence. Only a good woman takes the trouble."

Chauncey Boyne bowed, and as he moved, the light brushed a bluish sheen over his jet locks. He stiffened, neat-hipped, and spread his palms flat against the small of his back. A distant mood crept into his gray eyes as his mind sorted the decorations and orders. The regimental march that recalled the charge at Balaclava, for the Eighth had been there; important matters that had been part of his home schooling, as clear in detail as the minstrel songs his mother sang.

"Mother," he said, "why did we come to Virginia?"

Con Boyne flushed, and turned and glared at the telephone. Had it chimed then, the bell would have matched the tolling of a channel buoy of Innishowen Head.

Ellen Boyne closed the regimental case, taking plenty of time to make sure the latch was secure.

"Well, why don't ye tell the boy?" old Teigue demanded in his cracked-bottle voice.

"It would seem that with the war we should be back at Portglenone. Since I was born in Virginia, it may be difficult to join up with the Hussars," Chauncey added solemnly.

A stab of pain shot through Ellen Boyne. Old Teigue stared dully through the mists of fading glories.

"It's no time to be talking of the trouble." Major Boyne thumbed a wad of heavy shag into his pipe. "I'll have the War Office in a minute."

"Virginia's good for ye gran'ther's rheumatism," Ellen offered with vague simplicity.

"God save all here!" old Teigue bellowed. "So it's me rheumatism, eh? Fer that ye can bury me wi' a crutch in the coffin. Why don't ye tell the boy?"

"I was entitled to the medal!" Con Boyne stormed, and he blew a plume of smoke with the violence of an asthmatic colliery engine.

Chauncey turned to his mother for an interpretation. "A hasty gesture," she said, and sat down under the regimental case.

"Hasty?" the major exploded. "For four years and three months I applied. Decorations and Awards denied the claim."

"You were denied a medal, Father?" Chauncey recoiled as though a banshee had tossed dust in his eyes.

"Entitled to it, I was. Just a matter of papers." Con jabbed his pipe at some revolting figure in his past.

Again Chauncey appealed to his mother.

"Con was in America after polo mounts," she began.

"The year we won the Westchester Cup," Con added.

"Then came the war on August 4 and Con hurried back to New York, but there was no cabin available."

"So I took the train up to Boston. Same thing there," Con broke in.

"The Eighth was already mobilized and ready to go over," Ellen went on. "By now it was the retreat from Mons."

Con paced the floor. "In Boston I met a chap who'd been in the Boer War."

"What regiment?" Old Teigue broke in.

"The Lancasters. I told ye. He was a Lancashire man—wi' the King's and Queen's medals—four clasps. He told me they were shipping army horses out of Halifax, and that I could sign on and take them over."

"You worked your way over on a cattle boat?" Chauncey was aghast.

"I'm tellin' ye, the Eighth was mobilized and ready to go over," Con said testily. "So I signed on, and went home."

"There was a medal for that?"

"For thirteen days I was Mercantile Marine—feedin' horses on a cattle boat. When we docked at Liverpool, I never bothered to sign off or draw me pay. Just went down the gangplank and hurried to Lime Street Station."

"So he didn't get the medal," Ellen explained.

"Entitled to it, I was! I served on a government transport. Able-bodied seaman I was, and entitled to the Mercantile Marine medal."

"Ye were hasty," old Teigue muttered.

"The Eighth was mobilized on the Curragh!" Con stormed on.

"And for that we left Portglenone?" Chauncey was amazed.

"When a man's entitled to a medal, he should get it," Con rasped on, and stared at the telephone. "Thirteen days I served in hostile waters."

"Was it a smart medal?"

"Beautiful bit o' ribbon," Con answered his son. "Would come somewhere after the Mons Star."

"Before the Victory Medal," Ellen broke in.

"Whoosh!" old Teigue snorted. "A very small thing, to my way o' thinkin'. A cheap bauble designed for sweat-ragged seamen who stayed out of the Army. Ye'd put it up wi' the medals ye won wi' the Eighth? Pash!"

"If a man earns a medal, he's entitled to it," Con snarled.

"I'll see I get every one I'm entitled to," Chauncey said with an obstinate glare.

The telephone bell rang and after some cross talk Major Boyne said, "Right! Now let me speak to General Kilmayne."

There was a boisterous roar of recognition and greeting. Then Major Boyne said, "It's about Chauncey. I'm sending him over to join the Eighth, General. The lad can ride like any Boyne, an' I can get him there in no time. I'm expectin' ye to take care of him."

There was a long, melancholy silence. Finally Con wiped his brow with his handkerchief and wheezed, "Mechanics? . . . What would he be doin' as a mechanic?" Another stretch of sweat-wiping and throat-rumbling. "That's all, General. My deepest sympathy," and Con hung up carefully.

"Is the war over?" Ellen inquired.

"Worse! The Eighth Hussars are dismounted. They've been turned into an armored-car unit. They want only . . ."

There was a low sigh from old Teigue and he toppled from his chair.

For four days he lay and stared at the ceiling, and then passed on. "Ye'll bury me wi' me medals an' all," was the last thing he said.

Chauncey was the last to look on old Teigue's face and check the precedence of the medals before the big mauve lid was lowered. "It's not right," he murmured all the way to the plot. "All those medals."

When they came back, Chauncey walked out to the stables, and Tom Monahan said compassionately, "Ah, well, old Teigue had a full life."

"But the medals. It's not right they should be buried with him for none to see and know what he did. He had the Victoria Cross!"

"Ay, lad," Tom said, munching on a sprig of timothy. "Mayhap he had the V.C., but he's as dead as a felon on a gibbet. Mind ye, in all his eighty years it was about all he ever did, 'sides sponge on your father."

"He had the medals," persisted Chauncey.

"He niver lived up to 'em. A war's only a half-holiday in a man's life. Mayhap he enjoys himself, an' goes back to work. Mayhap he gets blind drunk an' rolls under a cart. It's as well old Teigue took his medals wi' him. He niver left nothing to display 'em against."

"Don't fret, Tom. I'll live up to mine, and I'll see I get 'em."

Chauncey Boyne changed his riding breeches and Newmarket leggings for the slacks and blouse of the Army Air Force, but he never imbibed the spirit. The classroom work was stock-whip agony, but he could fly like a man weaned on witch's milk. The primary flight training was as simple as taking a five-barred gate, but the book-slogging drained the suet, and he became taller, leaner, and blacker visaged.

"A dullard if ever there was one," Captain Hocking fumed as he studied Boyne's papers. "Never make a bomber pilot."

"Who would want him in a fighter formation?" Major Eggleston argued. "Where would he fit? Ever see him trying to play touch football?"

"He's the slickest aerobatic pilot ever turned out here. Who was that Spad guy in the First World War who won everything handed out, but couldn't stay in formation? A balloon-buster Joe who went out in a blaze of glory?"

"Frank Luke."

"Luke. I guess we'll never see another war like that."

"You will if you go along with this Boyne character," Hocking replied, and put Chauncey's name down for Mustang training. "He's decoration dizzy. Yesterday he asked me when he could put up his Good Conduct Medal."

The major and captain roared at the implication.

Overseas, Boyne experienced a series of new thrills, that added to the glory of the shoulder patch bearing the magic numeral "8," when he saw the RAF blokes in London with their neat strips of decorations under their silken wings. He would have given an arm for the double-wing setup of the old Eagle Squadron men who had served in the Battle of Britain.

There were fleeting moments when he regretted the mechanization of the Eighth Hussars, but later reflections assured him that there were greater opportunities to gather ribbons and other insignia of his heroism in the Eighth Air Force. He had already received permission to wear the European Theater of Operations medal and a blue patch under his wings to indicate he was a combat pilot. It would be only a matter of time before he

would have the Air Medal as a reward for completing five offensive missions. After that, in due course, there would be the
D.F.C., and then the Silver Star. Chauncey's mind flicked off the
rest, all the way up to the star-flecked sky-blue silk of the
Medal of Honor—the Purple Heart was never included in this
gaudy dream of gallantry.

Chauncey regretted that it had to end there, until he spotted
a Liberator pilot with the purple-and-white ribbon of the
British D.F.C. The explanation was simple and opened a broad
new field of possibility. The Liberator lad had been in the famed
Ploesti raid and had been included in a select group to receive
complimentary decorations at a Buckingham Palace investiture.

Chauncey reasoned that if the British, who were presumed
to be tight with their honors, recognized heroism and gallantry
as performed by other services, what about the Free French,
the Belgians, the Poles, the Czechs, and even the Norwegians?

Lieutenant Boyne tore around to Foyles in Regent Street and
bought a volume aflame with the medals and orders of the
Allied powers.

It was just a matter of time. . . .

But as Major Eggleston and Captain Hocking feared, Lieutenant
Boyne was a hot pilot over the field, but in a tactical unit he was
utterly worthless. Playing wing man to a more experienced
leader whose duty it was to go in and torch the Jerry 109's en-
crusted a scar of bitterness on the soul of Chauncey Boyne. On
his first mission he managed to secede from his formation and
disappear in a puff of cumulus cloud. Half an hour later he was
down on the deck with a trio of RAF Mosquitoes that were engaged in beating up a locomotive yard.

The Great Crusade was on.

On his second trip across the Channel he stayed put while
the Group escorted a flock of Forts to Bremen, but his ability
to get out of position drove his element leader crazy.

The next show saw the Mustangs over Dieppe, and again Lieutenant Boyne ducked the party and went off after a D.F.C. To

work that one, he faked radio trouble and dropped back. Ten minutes later he was jousting across the blue with two Me. 109's, and throwing ammunition all over the sky. His first pass was all mixed up with a fear that his wing camera would not function and that caused him to overshoot. The Jerry slid away and returned a long deflection shot that peppered Chauncey's tail assembly. The man in the Mustang swore, whipped over hard, and pooped off a series of long drags at a yellow-banded Mess-up, until he burned out the barrels of his guns.

"Boyne," Captain Clement warned him after interrogation, "we have a particular solo show for guys who won't stay in formation. It's a beaut! You'll get a special ship all your own."

"That's for me!" Chauncey beamed. "I just want to rack up a few Huns now and then. That's the only way a man can get anywhere in this war."

"You'll get somewhere, if you live."

"The tougher the better. You didn't get those decorations for formation flying, did you, Captain?"

Clement looked puzzled. "Is that all you figure on out here?"

"I didn't join up for the flying pay. What else is there?"

"There's a little matter of winning a war."

"We won't win it with neat formations."

"No, but a neat formation might produce the guy who will."

"I'll know him when I see him," Chauncey snapped. "He'll have at least four rows of ribbons up."

Clement studied this new specimen for a time. "I think you're our man," he said, and then added, "You know we lost Evans and Humbolt today, don't you?"

"Flak, wasn't it?" charged Chauncey, avoiding the captain's eyes.

"It could have been," Clement replied with cold accusation in his voice.

The next day the Mustangs were assigned to escort the bombers again, but Captain Clement gave no specific instructions to

Boyne, and Chauncey figured he was still brooding over the loss of his two fighters the day before. The target was Frankfurt, where there was plenty of flak, and Boyne whipped off just before the bombers began their run-in, and roared at three 109's that had been hanging around the periphery of the formation. Boyne heard Clement order him back, so he snapped off the set and concentrated on his personal crusade.

This time he nailed the first with a short, stinging burst that flamed the Jerry's engine. The second Jerry feinted retreat, and then came over tight and made a wild pass at the lone Mustang. Chauncey went boldly headlong at this assailant and scored by hacking away a Messerschmitt wing. It spun down, dragging a scarf of flame as the remaining wing wrenched off.

"What do they want?" he argued with himself. "I get two Huns on one show, and my next mission will be my fifth. That means an Air Medal at least. I ought to get a D.F.C. for those two 109's."

He hurried back alone, fretting over the possibility of a fouled wing camera and whether he would encounter any opposition to his claim of two victories. Then he thought of Ellen, and sang a wild Irish minstrel all the way home.

When he landed he noticed a new Spitfire, with unusual markings, on the apron in front of the maintenance hangar; but he was so anxious to buzz in and report his Huns that the matter soon drifted from his mind.

The Operations officer accepted the combat report with little enthusiasm but shot out a chit requesting the film from Boyne's wing camera.

"Is that all?" Boyne asked, perturbed. "I mean, I'll get credit for those two Huns, won't I?"

"It all depends. Oh, by the way, you're to report to the flight surgeon. Special assignment."

"Why? I've had all my shots."

"You got a beaut coming up," the Operations officer said.

"It's like this," the flight surgeon explained when they went into dinner that night. "From now on you eat at this table with me. You're on a special diet."

"What is this, Doc?" Chauncey pleaded.

"On high-altitude work there's no stuffing with hot dogs in the club grill. You go easy on bread and potatoes. No rich food or fats. At extreme altitudes, food that forms gas can tie a man in knots."

"Extreme altitudes? I've been on oxygen plenty, Doc."

"You're going plenty above anything you've ever done."

"I wish you'd give me a hint."

"I'm just responsible for you at chow, the rest is for the Intelligence and the Met boys to worry about."

The next morning, instead of going off with the regular mission, they boned him plenty on the F-52 camera, but Chauncey got little out of it; he just mooned about his Air Medal.

That's how it went for the next four days—just mooching around, watching the rest take off and straggle back; meal after meal with Doc sitting opposite, practically counting the calories. Then Intelligence came through with a ray of hope.

"High-priority job," Major Castleton explained. "You ever fly a Spit?"

"Spitfire? . . . You mean I get a liaison job with the RAF?" Chauncey beamed.

"Not exactly, although the RAF will be interested."

"I get to fly a Spit?"

"The one out in the maintenance hangar."

"Let's go!"

Chauncey was checked out on the British job, which was not too difficult since he had flown the Mustang; to all intents and purposes the two aircraft were identical. Chauncey spent one hour of glory whipping her through all the aerobatic tricks he knew, and checked the cockpit, instruments, and tank system.

He wondered whether he'd be eligible for the Victoria Cross, since he had been born in Virginia.

He brought the Spit in with a landing that dabbed like a touch of thistledown, and ran her back to the apron. The crew chief came out with a check sheet and stood by for orders.

"What about the gun button? There's no gun tit," Chauncey said as he climbed down.

"Guns? You ain't got no guns on this baby, Lootenant," the crew chief said with a grimace of puzzlement. "Didn't you know?"

"No guns?" quaked Chauncey. "I thought this kite was for a special mission."

"They's extra tanks where the guns was, Lootenant."

"I don't get it," Chauncey muttered, and threw back his black locks. "Rockets maybe?"

"No rockets, Lootenant. Just extra tanks."

"It's this way," Major Castleton explained after Boyne had fulminated all over the war room. "Tomorrow's the Big-B. Our bombers go to Berlin for the first time. Like your worrying about confirming those two Huns the other day, HQ will worry about what the bombardiers hit. They'll want the evidence on film."

"But that Spit carries no guns!" Chauncey exploded again.

"No. Just two cameras behind the pilot's seat. The Spit is perfect for this job. She's fast, handles beautifully at high altitude, and she's built to take two automatic cameras. All you have to do is take her there and get pictures of the bombing pattern."

"But no guns!" Chauncey moaned, and went off for another meal under the beady eye of the flight surgeon.

"You shouldn't need guns," the doc said. "You won't have to stay in formation, either. Take the fat off that pork chop."

The rest of the day Chauncey haunted the Operations room for news on his wing-camera film, but nothing had come through yet. He queried other pilots on what it took to get a

D.F.C. Did a man ever get one for two Huns on one show *before* he had completed five missions? How long did it take to appear in orders? No one was very helpful.

Chauncey went to the briefing the next morning with the rest of them. The Mustangs were to take the bombers only part way and then ramp off on a diversional mission. Long-range P-38s would pick up the Forts outside Berlin and see them out after the target had been spattered. If the timing was right, a Thunderbolt group would pick them up over Hannover and bring them home. Chauncey figured the Mustangs would have a milk run and maybe get a few Jerries. Just his luck!

Castleton charted Boyne's course and showed him photographs of check points along the route, and selected one target of opportunity—a point he could photograph if conditions permitted.

The Met Joe came in and chanted: "Ten-tenths low stratus cloud over the coast line, with cumulus built up to eighteen thousand feet. It should break up to five tenths over Holland, and he'll be in the clear a few minutes from the target. The wind will be ninety mph at thirty-five degrees."

"That's cutting it fine," Castleton grumbled. "Maybe he should take off early."

"Can't possibly send him off before twelve hundred hours," the Met man pointed out. "Even then he may run into some of the defense fighters following the bombers out."

"And me with no guns!" Chauncey groaned.

"You'll have no spare gas for any evasive action," Intelligence said. "We've got to time it so you get over Berlin just before the stuff closes in."

"I get credit for a full mission, don't I?" Chauncey queried. "I have an Air Medal coming up."

"For God's sake," gasped Castleton. "Is that all you think about? You're doing a hot photo show, flying about six hundred

miles at sub-stratosphere altitude, on a deal that proves or dis-
proves the efforts of about seven hundred men in bombers, to
say nothing of their fighter escort. It may resolve our whole
bomber policy. Isn't there some satisfaction in that?"

"If it's that important, it ought to be worth.... Maybe I
could get a Silver Star, eh, Major?"

The Intelligence man appealed to the Met Joe, but he had no
answer either.

Boyne was bundled off at noon, or about the time the bombers
would be easing around for their run-in on the Berlin target.
The Spit was loggy with her ponderous load of fuel, but once
airborne she behaved perfectly. Chauncey took the marked
course that avoided the restricted areas in Britain and started to
climb.

It began to get cold and he grumbled to himself about a
heating system that was trunked mainly to the all-important
camera wells. In no time low clouds blotted out everything
below, and he went on instruments, gauging the increasing wind
speed as he gained altitude. He should be in enemy territory now,
and his eyes swept from the retrospect mirror to all angles ahead.
Anything that appeared here could be only an enemy assigned to
intercept him.

No guns! His only hope—speed, flying skill, and the ability
to stay alert under the lulling purr of the Rolls-Royce engine and
the knifelike cold seeping through the cockpit panels.

The horizon ahead was marked, not by azure blue against
a rolling sweep of white, but a slim, gay strip of medal ribbons.

Chauncey assayed his chances. "With any luck I can get an
Air Medal for my fifth mission; maybe they'll have the film on
those two Huns which would get me a D.F.C., and a show like
this—they can't possibly figure anything less than a Silver Star."

He restrained a belch and wondered if he should have skipped
breakfast. It was hard to figure. He needed stamina to battle the
enervating influence of altitude and the strain of long flight. His

stomach rumbled again and he yanked at his cockpit and parachute straps to constrict his vitals.

Contrails swept frilly and white from his ejector exhausts,
which indicated crucial altitude—the twilight zone of air action.
A little higher, and he'd be in a position to spot the vapor trails
of enemy interceptors. If he dropped lower, he'd be in a position
to see the telltale streamers of the high-altitude defense ships,
while the Spitfire produced none.

The altimeter warned him to increase his oxygen flow; he
sensed his strength seeping away, and he recalled a line about
a pressure mask being able only to match the altitude of a fifteen-
thousand-foot mountaintop. Behind him the frost was finger-
thick on the camera housing.

Chauncey wondered why he felt so depressed. It couldn't be
just the altitude and the cold. He stared around at the vast half
globe of nothingness, and everything within him recoiled at a
fear he had not experienced before. The impact belted him for a
three-bagger.

And the radio taunted him. Someone off at a mere twenty-
five thousand feet was having fun. *"Look out, Ed. Bandits break-
ing off for your tail! Take him through and I'll follow you down.
...Three 109's, six o'clock....Let's go!"*

Someone was sticking, someone warmed with the excitement
of combat, someone racking up a citation.

"If I ever get out of this," Chauncey muttered, making sure
his transmitter switch was off, "they'll never get me on another
solo show! I never realized it before, but a man's courage expands
with the knowledge there's someone nearby to share or appreciate his danger. If there was only a Jerry to evade, flak to risk,
but there's nothing—nothing but a cold glare. I'm pinned up
here on the barb of a contrail like some squirming specimen on
a biology board. How can a man live up to his heritage under
conditions like this?"

He checked his instruments again and managed to jab a

penciled cross on his map. It was sixty below outside, and he
fumed over the instruments. Anything can go hoopla at that
temperature. He wondered if the wind had changed, and whether
he was still on course. There was no one to ask, no one to tell him.

Suddenly there was a break in the cloud carpet, as startling and
as ugly as a hole burned in a counterpane. He tried to identify
the area below, and wondered if it could be Hannover—his
target of opportunity.

There was no time now to audit. Through his numbed frame
a faint tingle of an alert aroused him. He checked the dials, sens-
ing something was wrong, but it wasn't on the panel. He swung
his eyes slowly around the distant horizon, but saw nothing;
yet the vibrating fear persisted.

A terror-stricken twist that gave a view over his tail completed
the pattern of dread; three Focke-Wulfs in tight formation had
slipped into the widening wake of his contrail. Castleton had
warned him about this trick, but he had fluffed it off. The
F.-W.'s were blending their own vapor plumes with those streaking back from Boyne's Spitfire and trying to slip up on him until
they were within firing range.

There was nothing to do but go out full bore. He punched
the throttle up the quadrant knowing he was eating up precious
fuel, but the risk had to be taken. No guns! In a few minutes
he had outrun them, and then the clouds opened wide and his
check point, a lake, sparkled below.

"Fifty miles from Berlin," Chauncey muttered, and watched
the Focke-Wulfs fall back and drop through the cloud carpet.
His relief was shattered a few minutes later when the engine
began to splutter. After several seconds of sweat-drenched
fear he switched over to the other wing tank and tried to figure
if he'd have enough even to make the Channel.

Below, Berlin appeared toylike under a watery glare of afternoon sunshine. The light reflected from the streets and roofs,
and through the coruscate design, warped columns of smoke

billowed lazily from the target areas. Slow clouds were seeping in, and for an instant Chauncey marveled at the timing Castleton and the Met Jo had bracketed for him.

He flipped his photo switch and prayed that the cameras were warm enough to respond. The white light smiled at him from the indicator panel. It was followed by an amber gleam, and as the shutters clicked off automatically, a series of green flashes reflected from the panel.

"White, amber, and green." Chauncey smiled reflectively as he held the Spit in level flight. "Same colors as the ribbon of the King's South African medal."

He completed his strip, and turned back through a thunderous barrage of flak. The cloud layer was creeping in, but he ran the cameras out—just in case.

"This can be a good deal," Chauncey muttered as he tried for a few more feet of altitude.

The trip back was cold but uneventful, except for a scare when he switched to his main tank. The fuel indicator refused to budge from the zero pin. For fifty miles he raged against his ill luck, thinking he had had a bad leak, but the engine continued to perk. Finally, when he was in sight of the Channel, the gauge defrosted and flipped back two notches. He had about twenty gallons in the tank when he circled his field.

That evening Castleton came charging across the mess hall; his face bore the illuminated expression of a man bearing top priority information. "Boy, you really got yourself a strip!"

"Medals? I'm not interested in medals," Chauncey responded with a wan smile. "What about the pictures?"

That stopped Castleton dead. He looked at Doc.

Doc said, "He's got a medal; his Good Conduct came through this afternoon."

"The film," Castleton beeped. "It's a classic! GHQ is nuts about it. The whole Group will get a citation! The pictures show they really did a job on Berlin."

"Holy smoke!" Doc said. "Now even *I* get a medal."

Castleton pulled up a chair and gripped the back of Chauncey's wrist. "The rest isn't so good, kid."

"I don't have to go back on formation, do I?" Chauncey wailed.

"Your Mustang wing-camera film—it's a dud. Your armorer forgot to take the lens cap off the camera. It's just blank."

"I can lick those Huns—*without* guns." Chauncey grinned.

"No Air Medal, either." Castleton piled it on. "Captain Clement rules you aborted on the Dieppe show. Claims he never saw you over the Continent. You still have only four missions racked up."

"So what? There'll be more raids on Berlin, and they'll need a guy to go and confirm it."

"That high-altitude stuff gets 'em," Doc said with a solemn glance at the Intelligence man.

"It got me," Chauncey said, and stared into space. "The last half-hour on the way back I sensed I was able to think clearer than I had ever done before. I felt I'd slipped off the foul bonds of earth. It was all so clean and untrespassed, I had to restrain the urge to open the canopy and put out my hand."

Doc said, "The Big Man up there would have shaken hands with you."

"High in that sunlit silence," Chauncey continued, "the sanctity of space, they call it, I was suddenly so glad I'd done what I'd been lucky enough to do. Nothing else mattered. I somehow knew I'd get back with the pictures, gas or no gas. If they'd given me a medal for that, I think . . ."

"No one could design a medal equal to—what you just said," Castleton mumbled thickly.

"Medals," Chauncey concluded, "are not always true symbols of a man's worth. Look at Doc here."

"Hey! Are you belittling my unit citation?" Doc stormed.

"No." Chauncey was flustered. "I mean, you've probably saved a hundred men's lives on this base alone."

Doc signaled to the waiter. "Let this kid have *two* pork chops tonight." He jerked his thumb at the rain streaking down the window. "Tomorrow's missions will all be scrubbed."

Torpedo Attack

No MATTER how often you come back," Ensign Claymore grumbled to himself down in the ready room, "you always have to go again." He snapped the catch of his lighter and applied the flame to the fourth pill in fifteen minutes. The gleam from the wick brought out the remoteness of his expression.

Lieutenant Commander Jiggs Glade was distributing mimeographed copies of their attack plans. Against the wall, the teletype provided a castanet accompaniment for the letters that danced across the ground-glass screen above.

The other men in the ready room were jotting down the stringy patter of flight data chalked up on a blackboard, trying to keep pace with the message tap-dancing across the screen. The group was made up of more than a score of faces; most of them were taut and stormy-eyed, a combination of fledgling excitement and sober resoluteness.

Pinky Claymore remembered the last time he had sat in a ready room awaiting the call: "Pilots, man your planes!"

That was five months ago; five months to the very day, and he was still an ensign. Five months ago he had scrambled up the ladder to the flight deck with the encouraging slap of Lieutenant Commander Hayes' heavy paw across his shoulder. Skipper Hayes had barked on the way up: "Whatever happens, Pinky, you stay with me. I'll see you get back, kid!"

Proof positive that you shouldn't make friends in a war. It's dumb, because you're always trying something screwy in an attempt to prove your friendship. The skipper was torched that day before they were anywhere near the Jap warship. A Zero picked him off and put a burst of tracer into his port wing tank, and Hayes had made no attempt to scramble out. Claymore wanted to turn back to see what happened when Hayes hit the drink, but they were at torpedo-attack level, and you can't turn in formation and hope to keep your wing tip out of the water.

Now Glade was talking in the ready room, saying exactly the same things the other skipper had said.

"This will be the first time for many of you. I haven't had much time to give you, but I've done the best I can. This may be a tough mission—if we find them. But no matter what happens, I want someone to put at least one pickle into that carrier. That's my final order—at least one in there. Good luck!"

The teletype cackled in derision and Claymore glanced up at the screen. He caught the last of the message and sensed what Glade was referring to.

"E-N-E-M-Y   C-A-R-R-I-E-R   F-O-R-C-E   N-O-W W-I-T-H-I-N   S-T-R-I-K-I-N-G   D-I-S-T-A-N-C-E. . . . T-I-M-E 13-0-0."

"Happy landings, guys!" Hayes had shouted as he had gathered up his flying gear. He'd winked confidingly and raised one eyebrow as much as to say, "Is that tellin' 'em, Pinky?"

This skipper was doing exactly the same thing. Glade was winking at Pinky. He'd given Claymore a section to lead. That was the most he had gotten out of that mess of five months before. He was still an ensign, and there wasn't a Navy Cross under his wings. Claymore guessed you had to go all the way to Tokyo to get the blue-and-white ribbon.

He erased the nervous smile from his face when Glade came along and said, "You must be getting a kick out of this, Pinky." He had no answer for that; his mind wasn't equipped at present to deal with subtleties.

"How do you feel, Pinky?" Glade asked as they wound their

way along the passageway to the ladder. "You don't mind going, do you? I mean, just getting back—and all that?"

"I'm all right," Claymore managed. He wondered if Glade knew exactly what "all that" meant. . . .

He'd been over it so many times with the newspapermen. He'd recited it again and again on the radio to boost the Crossley rating of word-weary news commentators who had described the battle as a Midway in miniature. "All that" had been told at the Men's Club at Eastridge between a pat of salty ice cream and a factory quartet that had attempted a gutting spiritual. The Rotary Club had given him a luncheon and a wrist watch for telling it. Someone had compared him to Ensign Gay and talked about the Midway battle again.

By the time he reached New York, he had it down pat, even to the laugh about Mickey Halford, who used to give imitations of Red Skelton over his radio while they were making circuits to come in. He'd told all that in Savannah, Toledo, Princeton, and even at a place called Buffer's Landing. There was always another close relative of someone somewhere who wanted to know just what had happened. Ten planes going west can leave a lot of curious relatives who desire the last possible drag out of the details. Twenty officers and enlisted men had taken off to get that Jap squadron, and only Pinky Claymore had returned— aboard a rubber raft.

It always ended up the same way, too. "You sure were lucky. How do you account for it? I mean to say, even your own radioman got it; but you got down and were saved."

In Pittsburgh a brother of a young radioman-gunner even questioned accusingly how one man out of twenty could get away safely.

"Did you go all the way in with them, mister?" he had asked. "I mean, did you actually attack her with *your* torpedo?" He had said that with a quarrelsome glint in his eyes and had cocked one thumb as though under the impression that a torpedo was fired from a derringer.

Pinky wanted to bust him in the jaw, but he just said, "No. We got it just before I was within range. Our engine broke up, and we just went down. I can't remember whether I discharged my torpedo or not."

So many points to explain, and now he was back with a torpedo squadron and going out again! The bull horn topside was bellowing and the loud-speaker was chanting orders while men, hampered with flying gear and parachute harness that made them walk with a rump-hitching stride, clunked across the island deck and stepped high over the water-tight doorframe.

"I wanted you to get a little more time in," Glade was saying. "Funny how we never seemed to get you on deck when there was a chance to do a routine. But I want you to take over Number Two section, because you've had experience."

Claymore blinked in the glare that spattered off the wings and cowlings of the fighters and torpedo bombers out there on the deck. He wriggled against the strain of his own misgivings, and agreed silently that he had had experience.

Five months before in that other show he'd had the experience of taking off from another carrier with nine other planes. The rest of the experience was a fantastic nightmare imprinted indelibly on his soul by the repeated demands for the details. He wondered again if he had always told it right. That is, had he ever added a few Zeros to the opposition, or in any way disclosed the biting fear that had clutched him with the cold tenacity of a pair of ice tongs? He wondered again whether he had told how Gillies and Honkie Walder had come together when Hayes was making that first feint attack. They'd never even had a chance to go in to glory—cold.

"It must have been a terrible experience," Mayo Knowlton had persisted that early evening in the Rainbow Room when they sat staring out across the blocked-up panorama of Manhattan. Mayo had worn a tiara of gardenias that held her bronze hair back from her creamy forehead. She had on an orange dinner dress with simple costume jewelry at the corners of the square neck. He could still see that dress and the saucy way the pleats were directed upward for the allure business. It was Mayo and all she meant to him that had first raised the question concerning his ever going again.

"I've got to put on five pounds," he explained with false enthusiasm. "Only five more pounds, and they'll let me go back."

Twenty hours on a raft floating about in the Pacific—he'd lost twenty-five pounds by the time he was convalescing in a naval hospital in San Diego.

She had placed her fingertips on his wings and leaned forward so that he caught the perfume of her hair and the warm affection of her breath.

"But, darling," Mayo had remonstrated, "they shouldn't send you back. There must be many others to take your place now. You can do so much good work here for morale—and recruiting. I mean to say, you have such a marvelous story!" She caught his pathetic smile and wondered if he felt she was acting childishly. She tried to buttress her fears and prove worthy of her place with: "But of course they will want you for leadership."

Leadership, with but one ring of braid on his sleeve! That was a laugh now. He was still an ensign and the nearest he had come to leadership was being burdened with a front position in Number Two section.

"If I can just pack on five more pounds," he repeated to avoid explaining the leadership business, "they'll pass me for active duty again."

If he hadn't met Mayo Knowlton that night at the old Whitelaw Reid mansion on Madison Avenue where they were having the Junior Officers' Ball, the question of his going back might not have taken on such terrifying importance. But it had, and now he was standing wide-legged against the flood of uncompromising light on the flight deck. The bull horn was bellowing again, and the ship's whistle screeched as the carrier swung into the wind.

"Baby, I'm sticking close to you!" little Packey MacInnes

was shouting at him. "Any guy who can do one pickle show and be the only one to get back will find me right behind his elevator all the way there and back."

"This'll be a joy ride, Packey. We have fighter escort *this* time," he said with mock assurance.

"Sure! We got fighters. Those guys will go off rat-racing the minute they spot trouble. They're just out here for the movies. I wonder..."

The bang and clatter of starting engines drowned out the rest. The plane handlers in their bright blue jerseys were hurriedly swinging the deep-bellied fighters out for take-off position, and the flight-deck officer was flagging them off.

Claymore tightened his belt another notch and thought of the trouble he'd had getting that five pounds back on. Actually, it had been something less than four and the flight surgeon at San Diego hadn't liked it a bit. "You're not ready, you know, Claymore." He had twirled his stethoscope in the correct movie manner. "You shouldn't be going back yet."

"But I feel all right, sir," Pinky had protested, a thick coating of furry fear impeding his speech. "I can rest plenty on the way out."

"I'm recommending that you do a stretch as navigation officer. That'll give you a chance to catch up. We don't throw off experiences like yours too fast."

"But that was five months ago, sir," Pinky heard himself remonstrating.

"I think we know best," the flight surgeon had decided with a flourish over his medical pad.

But there wasn't much rest flying out to Pearl Harbor; every mile was a spine-tingling measure of anxiety. Flying men seldom make good air passengers. There's a tormenting, repressed desire to charge up front and take over. Claymore worried about the navigation and chewed his fingernails down to the point where he could no longer get his teeth into them. By the time they were circling Diamond Head, his cheeks were drawn, his best whites were crumpled and stained from the oil-filmed cabin of the four-engined flying boat. The rest of the trip was endured aboard a cantankerous destroyer where his hard-earned four pounds were thumped off long before they made contact with the carrier off the islands of the Phoenix group.

Packey MacInnes was an irrepressible, small youth with funny legs. His radioman once said that Packey looked like a guy who had spent too many hours in a conga line.

"Look, Claymore," he bubbled through the tangle of his helmet gear. "I got a bet on with Monohan of Number Three. I bet him a can of metal polish that Number Two puts more torps in than his crowd. Wanna come in on it?"

"Metal polish?"

"Sure! You know—metal polish to shine up the medals we ought to get when we come back."

"You make the most of the dog tag you got on your wrist," Claymore said with a tinge of bitterness.

"Sure we'll get medals. How can we miss? The Order of the Wartless Pickle!"

"Look out you don't get fisherman's luck."

Ensign Claymore had been told that he would be cited and recommended for a medal when he was picked up that morning after the other scrap. Someone was always talking about medals—or promotion. All he had gotten was a wrist watch from a Rotary Club and a bid to a dance where he met Mayo Knowlton. They could have given him his lieutenancy and jacked his pay to thirty-six hundred—that would have brought Mayo closer.

The frenzied kick-over of propellers, the ranting of the bull horn, and the thump of fighters charging down the flight deck shook Pinky out of his depressing reverie. The talker on the bridge was bellowing apoplectic orders again as the half circle of putty-colored faces of the arrester-gear crew stared at him depreciatively.

"Man your plane, Claymore!"

Pinky stared about, and then realized he was alone. He hurried through the jigsaw puzzle of wing tips and whirling propellers until he saw an Avenger that had no pilot. His plane captain was standing on the wing root, huddled against the slip stream that torrented off Glade's torpedo bomber. Claymore signed the yellow acceptance sheet, handed it over, and tried to make himself comfortable. He hitched his belt, adjusted the seat for height, and glanced hurriedly over the spatter of instrument dials. When he jacked his helmet head-set in, the other crews were reporting through to Glade.

"How about it, Claymore? All set?"

"Number Two ready!"

Denning, his radioman-gunner in the back seat, was singing—something about apple trees being out of bounds for a certain young lady unless she was suitably accompanied by said Mr. Denning. The plane handlers were at the wing tips, awaiting their turn to swing the Avenger out into position.

"Number One section away!"

Glade led his pack down the white guide line that split the black teak deck. His motor thundered a salvo of exhaust off the metal walls of the island superstructure, raced on, and snipped off the steam posy blossoming from the flush-deck indicator nozzle. The torpedo-gorged Avenger dipped dangerously, once she cleared the lip, but Glade held her steady until she had picked up enough speed to make a normal climbing turn. The sunshine splintered from the gleaming metal and perspex hatch covers. Like magic the spinning wheels drew back with a coy flutter of panels and folded into their wells.

Two more Avengers followed down the deck, roared in unison as they turned, and then snarled with buzzsaw stridency to gain their position behind Glade. One by one they followed, each taking the plunge off the teak and dipping for the climb, and swinging around over the soapy wash of the escort destroyer that stood off the carrier's port beam. At four thousand feet they took up the prearranged formation and set themselves out in a Vee-of-Vees behind Glade's Number One section. Jiggs had asked Claymore about that, an hour before they had reported to the Number Three ready room.

"By rights," he had said, "we should go in line astern for a torpedo attack. That's what they say in the book, but from my way of thinking we're all in each other's way—or else we let the rear-position guys see too much. They can see too much, you know."

Pinky knew what he meant by that. If you attack in the last section and you spot three or four of your own outfit piled up in the sea ahead of you, you get an awful yen to pull out and flip the pickle from some ungodly distance.

"You guys went in—how?" Glade had asked. They were back on that again. Were they going to base all tactical strategy from now on on what had happened out at Midway?

"We started off in four sections of two with the skipper up front with a seventh. That's how we went in—what was left to go in. You see, we lost the skipper right off."

"Who took over?"

"No one! Hayes had told us right from the beginning to get a torpedo in—to get one in any way at all. I suppose we went in cold. Some got in—but they didn't get out. I didn't get anywhere near, except to see what happened."

"You mean they all went in cold—on the same side?" Glade pumped incredulously.

"Sure. We were being swatted like flies by the Zeros. We just went in for the first hunk of ship we saw."

Glade contemplated that scene, biting his upper lip and frowning. Then he washed it all out and began, "Now you see what I mean." He beamed at Pinky who was finishing his job on the charts. "We go in—if we find her—and I'll take our portside elements in on their portside. You clear on signal and take our starboard gang around her stern and—well, we'll give them two sides to protect."

"You mean you want me to lead half the squadron and take them in? But I've never even led a section!"

"Why not? You've had the experience in an attack. You've been through it and come out. That's what counts. Me—I've only done practice run-ins. I've never been off the deck with a live pickle!"

Pinky tried to make the shutter of his understanding keep up. He sorted the words and tried to remember when they first started calling a torpedo a pickle. He tried to remember how many rings of braid a lieutenant commander sported on his sleeve. Something about adding half a ring, or was that a lieutenant, junior grade? Funny how he couldn't remember. But he knew there were section leaders who were lieutenants, junior grade, in their squadron who should be burdened with the responsibility of taking on the starboard elements. Wasn't it enough that a guy had taken over the navigation?

There were all sorts of details to be gathered from air plot and carefully sorted and diagnosed. There were temperature, dewpoint, nearest land and recognition signals to clarify. The flight surgeon at San Diego had said he would do a stretch as navigation officer to give him a chance to catch up. Showed how much shore-based medicos knew about staff work aboard a flattop. The bridge navigation officer was one guy—a very large guy with a commander's braid on his sleeve. The navigation officer of a torpedo-bomber squadron was something else entirely—and he wasn't a commander.

Ensign Pinky Claymore wished the skipper hadn't picked him to lead the starboard attack—it brought up memories of Mayo Knowlton and her Rainbow Room ideas about leadership....

They caught up and set out their Vee-of-Vees behind Glade's spearhead of four. All this was simple, but as the miles sped below them, the dancing film of the other torpedo attack jerked through the unevenly spaced frames of his mind's projector; there were fighters and scout bombers in the scene somewhere, but the fighters would not be able to accompany them very far.

That's the way it was before. They all took off and the pattern in the sky looked like a descriptive illustration in one of the photographic weeklies that proves how easy it is for an air service to gang up and wipe out the opposition. Why wouldn't those guys who drew the pictures take time to figure out range of action and tankage?

Glade's voice came over the radio again. The skipper shouldn't be doing that. They were supposed to observe radio silence as long as possible, but Glade was new, in spite of his two-and-one-half rings.

"If we spot the enemy units," he repeated, "we maintain our present formation until I give the final order. I'll hold that. Section leaders report."

One by one they responded and gave the recognition signal. Packey MacInnes couldn't resist another gag to Claymore before they snapped off. "Don't forget, Claymore, I'm with you. If you don't bring me back, you'll have to answer to my mother. She's a firebrand!"

"Pipe down, MacInnes!" Glade ordered.

Another mother to answer to, Pinky reflected. That was another drawback to this business. Too many mothers who asked too many questions. There was Pelotti's mother in Detroit who demanded over and over what had become of Tony's wrist watch. She'd given it to him at Christmas with an order not to wear it if there was any danger of its being damaged. Pelotti had dutifully written and assured her he *never* took it with him on patrol missions. Someone ought to know what became of it. There was a pecuniary-sentimental value to it now.

Husdren's mother really nailed him down. She was a limpid lavender female who reminded Claymore of a funeral spray, and she had arranged the interview with all the gloomy deliberation of a mortician; the shades were drawn and an old clock gonged somewhere along a Stygian hall. Claymore had squatted gingerly on the edge of a creaky horsehair chair, twirling his cap in his hands.

Mrs. Husdren had sat down, straightened her skirts, placed an elbow on the arm of her chair, carefully mounted her facial cameo in the prongs of her osseous fingers, and commanded sepulchrally, "You may now proceed, Ensign Claymore."

When he had finished she arose, carefully raised the shade, and concluded, "Thank you. Charles was always a good boy. He always did as he was told. I suppose you could do with a drink?"

That was the closest Ensign Claymore ever came to getting drunk. After that he told the story right. He really liked Mrs. Husdren.

The Avengers roared along the prescribed course for more than an hour. The Wildcat fighters stormed up, circled ahead, and then raced back for their floating base. The scout bombers swung off on another course, and the torpedo planes were alone.

Denning commented on that over their intercommunications phone, and Claymore explained that there probably wouldn't be anything doing.

"Did you have fighters with you in that other scrap, sir?" Denning's voice seemed to be coming off an old wax record and for a minute Claymore had to reassemble the words and place them in their proper time bracket.

"Sure, we had fighters with us. Zeros—but plenty!"

"But you got that big Jap cruiser."

"Someone did," Claymore agreed abstractedly. "Someone got in. We never found out who. I suppose I should know, but it didn't seem to matter then."

"No. What does it matter, so long as someone got her?" the radioman agreed as he checked the formation.

Pinky was startled by that. He pondered on Denning's philosophy, and wondered why Denning took the long view of it. Denning, just a radioman second class, drew down about ninety bucks a month—maybe. He was taking plenty of risk aboard these tin-fish carriers. Funny about guys like Denning. They plug away like hell and annoy everyone from the skipper down to get a flight rating. Ashore, they're just gobs. You can't tell them from the pharmacist's mates or the signalmen when they're scrambling for the liberty boat. What the devil did they see in just having "ARM 2/C" after their names? The public which has been spoon fed on the glorious deeds of the ace pilots simply can't assimilate the fact that a man may take the air, ungilded with the braid of commissioned rank. But Denning had said, "What does it matter, so long as someone got her?"

Claymore turned in his seat and looked at Denning and tried to figure what lay behind that heavy-featured face. The radioman stared interrogatingly with his eyes for a second, and then smiled. It was a sincere, substantial smile that lit up his whole face. Claymore reflected quickly that it was really a smile, not a grin, and he felt it had loosened something that had constricted his chest for weeks.

"You got any metal polish in your sea bag, Denning?"

"Sure. I guess so, sir."

"Good! Stick with me, kid; maybe you'll need some."

"I don't get it, sir."

But the earphones were jangling again, and Glade's voice came back from the spearhead unit. He was reporting three enemy observation ships and several columns of smoke just ahead. That was for the air officer's information back aboard the carrier.

Denning slapped him across the shoulder blades and mumbled something about Zeros upstairs.

Glade's wings were being waggled, and the lead section was going down stiff for the torpedo-attack level.

"There's a flock of Nips upstairs, sir!" Denning was yelling.

"Okay! Okay! They're all yours," Pinky conceded.

Glade's voice came over the set again. "We'll take the carrier first. There's a light cruiser ahead, and four destroyers for escort. We'll take the flat top."

Denning's guns began a mad racket, and the same old feeling of *this is it!* enveloped Pinky. He sat tense, stiff with the pressure of the dive, his nose bloated with the force of the compression set up under the closed hatch. He wondered if he would black out when they leveled off.

Glade was talking again, selecting his words carefully. "I'll take the portside elements in direct. The starboard elements will attack behind Claymore of Number Two.... Repeat, Claymore."

The antiaircraft was thudding its percussion chorus, and they charged through the concussion and smoke. Claymore managed to repeat the order between bursts by Denning, who was tripping short jolts of .30-caliber stuff at the Jap fighters.

"Take it away, Claymore!" was the last he heard from Glade.

Three Zeros sliced past when Pinky waggled his wings and took the starboard element away. They were down low now, and just skimming the chrome-plated waves.

Here it was again. Zeros, and a great wall of metal ahead—a wall of metal that flicked and spat flame. An Avenger came out of a smoke blob, completely out of control, raged at the sea, and went skimming blindly on its belly, leaving a series of circular dabs, until it caught a wing tip. Then it cartwheeled over and exploded.

The Zeros were screeching down from above, their rifle-caliber tracers selecting the bead for the heavier crump of air-cannon shells to follow. Denning yelled something, and a flame-scarved mass of dural and smoke plunged into the ocean a few dozen feet ahead of Claymore's flailing prop.

"Take it, line-astern, starboard elements!" He spoke clearly into the throat mike. Then he remembered, and added, "Watch out for the spurts put up by their main batteries."

He wished he had borne down on that to Glade before. He hoped Glade would have caught it. It was the old Jap trick to direct their big guns at the sea ahead of them. He was glad he had remembered that.

"Go ahead, sir!" Denning yelled. "They're all with us."

"We'll need a lot of metal polish—if we make it. Who got that Zero?"

"What does it matter?" Denning began his routine again.

"Remember, Claymore," the voice of Packey MacInnes came over the set. "I'm with *you*, baby."

Pinky signaled and made his turn over the two trailing Jap destroyers, and then glanced quickly across at the carrier. He saw several Zeros beetling along its deck, and then he choked on a dull cry.

The lead Avenger of Glade's element slammed headlong into a geysering spout of water that came up from a low-angled five-incher. The hapless plane smacked into the climbing column of green and white; Pinky saw the wings break away and skim forward past the column of water and go skipping across the shrapnel-spiked rollers with the abandon of two skimmed stones.

He closed his eyes and remembered that Glade was leading that element. Glade should have watched out for that spurt business. That's where experience counts. Now, because Glade had not appreciated that danger, Pinky was left in full charge; this was the leadership that Mayo had burdened him with in New York.

This was it! This was what he came out of the other scrap for. No extra braid, no gay ribbon of blue and white. Just an extra load of responsibility. Leadership; but Denning would say what did it matter who got it, so long as someone got it?

Good man, Denning.

Pinky knew what was expected of him now, braid or no braid. The others had never seen this sort of thing before. Each one was watching *his* wing tips. He had to go through with it. He couldn't sneak out, because he had to show them how to avoid shell spouts. They wanted to see how it was done—with a live pickle aboard.

The thud of heavy ack-ack and the whiplash of pom-poms

piled up the opposition against him. He nosed down a foot or so lower and risked his prop tips. The guns in the main batteries were belching and sticking serpent tongues of flame through the bolsters of smoke. He zigzagged and warned them again, and then assumed the brunt of command.

"*Torpedo attack!*"

Good God! The mad, screaming obbligato was big enough now, and they must have passed through the worst of it. There had to be a law of averages; some of them had to get away. You can't lose ten every time.

He saw the five-inchers flick flame again, and he pressed the rudder and changed course. A clutching fist of sea exploded off his port wing tip, reached up—and missed! He held it, and saw the full details of the carrier's great hull. An Avenger screeched and came up in a sliding zoom from the other side, and Pinky changed course back again as another bellow of rage roared up on the starboard side.

A Zero charged at him, and Denning's guns met it head on. The Jap fighter jerked, nosed down, struggled to recover, and fouled a wing tip.

"Base over apex!" commented Ensign Claymore.

The great wall of Mitsubishi steel was rushing toward him now. He waited another second, then punched the torpedo-release button. The Avenger leaped joyously with relief from the load. Pinky hunched up in his cockpit and continued on, holding the dancing warplane down until he could see the porthole detail in the plates of the hull. Then with a low cry he brought the stick back and ripped her up over the depressed stacks. He banked sharply to clear a stubby mainmast, glanced back, and saw a steely-white gash hissing toward the carrier.

He was in the clear and leveling off before the torpedo smacked in.

"Someone got one home, sir!" Denning reported as he champed on the oily thumb of his glove. "You really did a job, sir."

"Someone had to, Denning. The law of averages—and experience, y'know," Ensign Claymore explained.

Eleven battered war planes re-formed behind Claymore's torpedo bomber. They circled and stood off while the enemy carrier reeled and walloped through the wreckage-strewn rollers with what headway she had left. The Zeros sought sanctuary on the deck of a mother ship that could offer no succor. The escorting destroyers moved in to stand by and pick up the survivors who were already abandoning ship and slithering down over the explosive-battered torpedo bulge.

"Well, we did the best we could," reflected Ensign Claymore. "Next time I'll have had more experience. We'll have to go again —of course."

Night Fighter

CHRISTMAS DAY—1944.

Only just! A few minutes ago it was Christmas Eve somewhere outside Saint-Omer. Charley Burke tried to remember when he'd been away from home on Christmas before.

Christmas Day.... *Joyeux Noël* it said on those Christmas cards he had bought somewhere over here. Charley never could remember the names of towns anywhere but in the state of New Jersey.

Someone was celebrating! The parcels and packages were coming up in high-explosive canisters, and the decorations were eye-searing fire balls that were shackled together with tinseled chains of entangling hate. They seemed to ride along with them, somehow keeping a certain distance, and Charley blinked and wondered if his peepers were going back on him.

He had spoken to Lieutenant Green, his navigator-gunner, about them, but Green had simply noted that he *had* observed them. That was Greeny—just because he had a commission, Burke figured. It really scalded Greeny to have to fly behind a warrant officer—Flight Officer Charles Burke of Jersey City. At least that was the way Charley thought about it.

"I never saw nothin' like that before," he said with finality, and Lieutenant Green winced—as he always did at Burke's grammar.

"I presume they're a new version of the old flaming onion. Interesting, but not particularly troublesome, if you leave them alone."

Charley felt that Greeny was putting on an act. It was the way he made things seem so easy.

"I heard about 'em," Charley muttered over the intercom, "but I never seen them before. I guess this is something special for Christmas, eh, Greeny?"

Lieutenant Green did not object to Flight Officer Burke's addressing him as "Greeny," once they were airborne, but on the ground—even though warrant officers were accorded certain privileges in the officers' club—he demanded his rightful respect, living up to the code and carrying out the spirit of his graduation pledge, as he interpreted it. Here, where they composed the two-man specialist crew of a Black Widow, he was willing to be broad-minded in the matter.

He peered out the high-arched plexiglas canopy above his navigation table and considered the dancing fire balls as they appeared to maintain the same relative position, despite the fact that the P-61 was really batting out the knots.

He wondered whether this was an optical illusion, or whether it was another Jerry secret weapon.

"So long as we maintain course," Green said, "I don't see how they can harm us."

"But suppose we make a turn?"

"That's what I'm wondering about."

"Why don't you put a burst into that string out there and see what happens?"

"No, I think not. First of all, we'd indicate our presence. Secondly, we can only see the fireball part in this darkness. No telling what might be connected with them."

Charley considered that as he checked his compass. He hadn't thought of it, and it needled him to think that Greeny would. But that was Greeny, always playing it safe, being conservative. Still, in this instance, he *could* be right.

They were flying south out of Liége and heading for the pig-snout design hurriedly washed in on Lieutenant Green's chart; it was startling how much like a pig's head the Belgian Bulge

had become in the past nine days. Looking below, the salient
points of the image could be imagined with little effort, because
of the jets of gunfire, the raddled smudge of burning villages,
and the glare of torched supply dumps. One might even point
out that the pig was smoking a fat, rosy-tipped cigar.

That would sound funny in a report, but the glow of the
stogie was Bastogne, and there was nothing funny about the
fact that thousands of Yanks were trapped there. Trapped and
praying for the supplies they hoped would come from the black
skies—supplies that they trusted would be dumped from the big
bellies of C-47 transports, C-54 Skymasters, or, in fact, anything
capable of getting a few pounds of defensive necessities into
the air.

Half an hour before, Burke and Green had taken off on a tactical mission designed to block off enemy night fighters who
might interfere with the sky trains. They had been at this for
nearly a week, daring the flak, the fire balls, and the weather.
Even now they were operating under conditions that would
deter a sea gull. But what was a Black Widow or two, carrying
a crew of two men, compared to Bradley's forces holding up
the Huns in Bastogne?

Lieutenant Green had had plenty of time to think about it.
He'd first begun to consider it long before he was told at Valdosta,
Georgia, that he'd never make the pilot grade. The captain had
been splendid, and Green had accepted the decision. As a matter
of fact, he had felt a great load lifted from his shoulders—and
his soul.

"I'm sorry about this, Green," the captain had said. "You
seem to have everything to make a good pilot. But that's the
trouble. You have too much."

"Too much, sir?"

The captain tapped his temple. "Too much here. It's your
imagination. The *way* you think." He brought out a sheaf of
yellow sheets, flipped them over one by one, and smiled.

"These flight sheets, Green. Page after page of what you *thought* when you were in the air. Now, don't get me wrong. This has nothing to do with your nerve—your courage. Each of these sheets is a treatise on what can happen to an aircraft in the air. Beautifully written and sound in detail."

"But I thought, sir . . ."

The captain waved a friendly hand. "I know—I know. Some of us on the board here felt you were trying to be sincere—to show how you were interested in ignition systems that were not perking, to help the maintenance department ferret out the trouble, or even to indicate that you were really interested in the mechanical side of this business."

Green would have attempted to argue further, but he knew those yellow sheets had betrayed him; words set down in a fine round hand, each another unit of guilt against him; words proclaiming his innermost fears, set in terms of tankage, fuel pressure, torsional strain, structural failure. . . .

The voice of the captain aroused him: "But we feel that you are too valuable a man to be thrust aside. The board, after careful deliberation, has decided to use these penetrating talents of yours. You still want to fly, I presume?"

Preston Green answered automatically, and because he had breeding. A question is always answered, and, if possible, complimentarily to the speaker.

"I'm glad to know that." The captain doodled with a ten-dollar automatic pencil. "We are just starting a new course to train certain specialists—navigator-gunners for our night-fighter crews. Your navigation is excellent, and in the air—at night—you will be able to give full play to your talent for thoroughness without distraction from the outside—the darkness, I mean. You'll be commissioned, of course. Will you sign here, please?"

Green signed the card, stood up, saluted, and walked out.

A little later on he wondered about that. Instead of shielding his imagination from distractions, the darkness only accentuated them.

He was still wondering when the Black Widow swerved with brutal suddenness, and Green winced as his mind raced through the series of strains and stress factors involved. Every spar, cable, and fitting seemed to be bolted to something bunched with nerves inside him, and he only just clamped his teeth firm on a throat-slitting yell.

Burke was swinging into a dagger-winged shadow that was dragging a streak of snubbed flame.

"There's one. Will you take him, Greeny?"

"I'll take him."

Lieutenant Green snapped on the remote-control gear and set the servo-amplifier mechanism that operated the flexible gun turret high amidships. His mind traced the course of the electric impulses that charged through the secret mechanism. The Black Widow banked sharply again and Burke moved into a position parallel in flight to the enemy.

"Don't take too much time!" Charley remonstrated.

Green took aim, and fumbled with the trigger switch. He still allowed his mind's eye to travel through the mechanical sequence of the remote-control sight, his fears building up like the pressure in a hydraulic ram. The possibility that somewhere along the line the mechanism could foul, drained all the confidence from him.

"What you waitin' for?" Burke yelled.

Green wondered whether the fire interrupters would function and prevent the swinging turret from pouring two ripsaw streams of metal into their own tail assembly; whether the turret mechanism was answering the little device before him, whether it was turning and responding to his request for less elevation, to swing to the left. In training he had been sure of it, but this was entirely different. Here he wasn't sure. He couldn't *see*. You can't trust what you can't *see!*

Talent for thoroughness, without distraction from outside affairs—hell!

At last he mustered the courage to press the trigger switch. Everything was right! The lines crossed properly! The bubble was centered and the image properly proportioned on the scale.

The guns spat out and tried to lace the two aircraft together with reins of golden tracer over the humped canopy of the German, but the fire disappeared in abortive splutters toward what he knew to be Saint-Hubert.

He *knew* Saint-Hubert was over there, but he never knew what was going to happen when he pressed that trigger switch. Dicing with what you *knew*, against your hopes, and somehow you always lost.

"He got away!" Charley growled. "You missed him by feet. There he goes, dead below us. I should have taken him."

"Right! You should have taken him. Why didn't you?"

Charley didn't answer. He was winding the Black Widow back on course for their plot over Bastogne. They had an area to sweep for more than an hour, and he was trying to live down the fact that he was flying a Black Widow instead of a Thunderbolt.

Ninety seconds later a great glare lit up the sky around them. It took the form of a giant candle flame at first, and then stretched itself out to a long scarf of smoky gold to mark the final gesture of a C-47 going down in flames.

"We should have nailed that guy," Burke said stolidly over the intercom. "It's too late now. He got away!"

"You should have taken him," agreed Green. "You have heavier stuff on your stick."

They watched the torch wriggle down to hit in the wood outside Houffalize.

"Yeh, I should've taken him," Burke mumbled, "but I was tryin' to let you take the ball for a change."

Charley hoped Greeny would never know what he meant. Lieutenant Green might have access to the records, if there were such things over here. There might be papers somewhere that told about it. The thoughts of records and papers haunted Charley, because they were unintelligible and frightening—like a report card from school.

No one could accuse Charley Burke of imagination, but he had dreams. God, what dreams he had! Night after night—when things were going wrong. The dreams had everything—taste, smell, and substance. The taste was in his mouth when he woke up. The smell came from the tang of new varnish on a broad-surfaced desk and the choking odor of official paper, typewriter ink, and the stench of a cigar on the captain's desk that morning. Burke never smoked a cigar after that, not even when butts were short at the PX....

The substance was the barrel chest of the captain and the two rows of ribbons. Real ribbons, too, and you can't argue with a guy with that stuff up. Burke knew he'd "had it" the minute he opened up with that football routine.

"Oh, come in, Burke," the captain had called, and then tucked his left sleeve into his blouse pocket. "Sit down, will you?"

The papers rustled until the typewriter ink billowed up in a strangling storm, the cigar smoke tightened the knots and folded the ends away.

"Ever play any football, Burke?" the captain began, without looking at him.

"Yes, sir. Ain't it there—in my papers?"

Papers, cards, and records had to have something good in them. Burke hoped for the best, but he felt like a featherweight taking on Joe Louis.

"Oh, yes, you played high-school football in Jersey City. I guess you had a pretty good team there."

"We had a good club, but we didn't get nowhere much when I was there."

"You look like a backfield man."

"Yeh, I played roving ball, but I only played two years."

"Oh, have to quit school?"

"No, sir. The coach—we just didn't get along."

"But the team—after that?"

"Practically the scoreless wonders." Charley grinned. "You wouldn't believe it, sir, they won the state championship."

"Amazing!"

"Never could figure that out," Burke said, wading in up to his chest. "How did you know, sir? That ain't in my records, is it?"

"No. I guess you never told anyone before, either."

"No, sir! I never could figure that out."

"Ever think that these scoreless wonders somehow always win state championships because they never let the other side score?"

Charley was leery now. There was a familiar twist to this. "I expect that's what it adds up to, sir."

"And if you stop them from scoring, you must have some defense."

Burke was perspiring now, and he wished the captain would douse the stogie.

"But you have to score, once, at least, if you want to win," Burke protested feebly.

"I know. I used to play football. I saw many a game won by some kid snatching a goofy pass or picking up a fumble."

"Jees, sir! That's just how these guys won—that year!"

"You ever get away with a play like that, Burke?"

"No, sir. I guess I wasn't too hot, defensively."

The captain shoved the papers away. "That's why I called you in today, Burke. You won't do for Thunderbolts."

"I—I won't do, sir?" Burke felt his world drop out from under him. He instinctively fumbled for the latch of his safety belt. The charts and maps on the wall slithered into each other, and the globe on the bookcase whirled and swept away half a man's life span in a few seconds.

"Don't get me wrong. We're not washing you out."

"But I won't do—for Thunderbolts—sir?"

"You won't do for the work involved. You have no sense

of teamwork, and forgive me if this sounds like cheap preaching."

"You mean—defensively?"

"I mean teamwork as a whole. Perhaps it would be better summed up in the term *sacrifice*. You're not willing to sacrifice yourself for the rest of your formation. I mean, you'd go kiting off, knocking down Huns when you should be playing your defensive part—saving another man in your own outfit."

Charley tried to fight it out. "Where do you get all this stuff, Captain?"

"Through obvious channels. Your own reports, for instance. Your flight leaders, who are trained observers in this work, all reach the same conclusion. You show it, not only in the air, but right here on your squadron teams. You're still playing a roving half in Jersey City for a fellow named Burke. You asked for it. I'm handing it out."

"That's kinder tough to take, sir."

"You're a lucky man! I wish someone had told me—years ago. I wouldn't have traded this"—the Captain flicked at his empty sleeve—"for these," and ran a very clean forefinger across the two rows of ribbons, "had I been jerked up at the right time." Then he added, "It wasn't worth it."

"I don't get that, sir."

"I was a grandstander, too, Burke. I hit fifteen Huns and some ribbons, but I lost a whole flight many a time. And I almost went myself because someone else played the same game. I was lucky, at that."

"I think I understand, sir."

"No, you don't. You won't understand until you get in a jam —and squeal your guts out, as I did."

"But can't you give me a try?"

"No. We'd never know whether you had learned, until you'd let a flight or even a squadron down. It's too late then."

Burke felt he ought to bawl, but somehow he couldn't force a tear. He'd heard about that—not that it ever worked—but he couldn't manage a noticeable blink.

"That's that, Burke. It won't be too bad. There's another place for you where perhaps your particular trait can be utilized to the full."

"But I should think—on single-seater fighters, sir . . ."

"There you are! You haven't the foggiest idea of the work. You signed up to become a glamour boy. A war ace. We just can't use you, Burke."

"But someone has to shoot the Krauts and Japs down."

"Fine. You're going to get all the chance in the world. We're transferring you to night fighters—Black Widows. That's your league, Burke. You'll be responsible only for yourself—and your navigator-gunner."

"I'll have another man with me?"

"Special crews are being trained for the job. It will require some teamwork between the two of you; and that's the least risk we care to take with fellows like you."

"Night fighters! Jees!"

"Don't get me wrong. Not all Black Widow pilots are like you. They're all damn' good pilots—first off. Some are selected because they have cats' eyes—good night vision. Others prefer this lone-wolf prowl with someone they can trust. Here and there we find a man like you who needs to learn the meaning of teamwork and personal sacrifice."

"Yes, sir! That will be better—than nothing."

"Good. Then you'll sign here?"

Charley Burke signed and walked wide-legged from the room.

Lieutenant Preston Green knew the setup was wrong. He watched where the burning transport hit, and marked another scarlet cross against his spotty record. He crouched and glared at the bewildering instrument, supposed to link him with glory. It was a beautiful piece of intricate mechanism, but to Lieutenant Green it was just that.

Remote gun control!

Remote as hell! Perfect in practice and theory—until you

needed it. The whole idea was too involved. The last link with actuality stripped from him. Here, he couldn't even *touch* the guns; they were aimed and operated by remote control. He was part of the war, but not of it. He wondered whether, after hostilities, there would be a special designation for the men who fought—by remote control. In his bitterness he ranked them only a few notches above the conscientious objectors.

He glanced at the hunched shoulders of Flight Officer Burke. The gleam from the fire balls brought out the harsh expression of his eyes. They still dangled or raced along with them, reminding Green of the ridiculous chemical symbols used to designate the formula of some mysterious brew—like penicillin or nylon.

It was all right for Burke. He wore pilots' wings. He had something in his hands besides a pencil and protractor. His hands actually operated controls—controls that were not remote. When he shoved the stick forward, he got visible results. Same thing with the throttle, the landing gear, and the flaps. He could sit and change the pitch on the props, and feel the responses through his gloves, and experience the electric thrill of—command!

That was it. Burke had command!

Sitting behind a remote-control gunsight was like pressing a button in the White House and the next day reading in the paper that you'd opened a world's fair. . . .

The Black Widow retched through another sharp bank, and Green caught Burke grinning at him over his shoulder. The sequined world below tilted on its side.

"Making the turn," Burke reported.

"Roger. Make it eight minutes this time. We'll turn again over Neufchâteau."

They held a steady course now, passing the western outskirts of Bastogne, which was burning and stewing in its Gethsemane. Green jabbed a dot on his chart and penciled in the time figures from his chronometer.

"I don't like those fire balls," Charley grumbled.

"Don't worry about them, as long as they don't bother us."

"They bother me, and I can't do anything about them."

"Neither can the swine who sent them up. Apparently they don't even have remote control."

Burke pondered on that. "You don't like that gadget, do you, Greeny?"

"No. I find myself tracing the sequence of operation whenever I use it. I can see where so many malfunctions can occur."

"Yeah. You got too many things to think about in your racket. I'd go nuts."

"Someone has to do it."

"I wouldn't get much satisfaction out of that."

"Well, stay away from those fire balls. They could be bad news."

"Don't they know *anything* about them?"

"If they do, they're not telling us."

"For my dough, they don't know nothin'!"

"Well, don't fall for them—until we do know."

"It must be hell to have to fly with another guy," Charley began again after a short inspection of the horizon.

"It's not too bad with a pilot like you," Green pointed out. "You're all right.... And then, we all have to make some sacrifices to the war effort."

"Sure," the pilot agreed after a swallow. "We all gotter make sacrifices."

"At first I didn't mind being washed out as a pilot. There was a minute or two when I was glad."

"Glad?"

"I guess I was slated for B-17's. Then I got to thinking about all the others I'd be responsible for."

Charley argued: "But remember you would have had a copilot, in case you fouled one off."

"I suppose I saw him as another man I was responsible for."

"I wouldn't. I kinder like the idea that maybe you *could* fly this thing if you had to." Then Burke qualified the statement

with, "Even though maybe you could only get it back somewhere over our area. A guy could bail out then."

"And not have to risk one of my landings?"

"That, and turning her over to you, Greeny. I don't know."

"I don't know either. I'd really like to know. Right now I'd
give all I have to be as good a pilot as you, Burke."

"Yeh. My only responsibility is you."

The conversation seemed unreal, coming over the intercom,
and Green was at loss for an answer. He looked at Burke's
hunched shoulders—and just wished.

"But I guess I was wrong on that, Lieutenant." Green looked
up at that "Lieutenant" routine. "I mean, I guess we got a hell
of a responsibility to those poor guys down there, as long as we
are up here, eh?"

"See what I mean?" Green said.

"I see something—Kraut fighters! What do you say—just
about two o'clock, slightly below us."

"I see them, but watch out for those fire balls," Green warned.

Burke was a man of action. The Black Widow screwed over
hard, her snout headed straight for a series that dangled and
swung enticingly.

"You're sticking your chin out, Burke," Green started to say.
"Why cut in that way?"

A fire-studded hammer crashed in one side of their nose; the
Widow seemed to have collided with an obstruction that col-
lapsed only after seconds of furious storming. The scream of
outraged metal, attuned to the screech of pain from Burke, shot
a bolt of fear into Green's brain. It all happened in a jagged unit
of compressed time, and Green felt that something with cruel
metal points had exploded inside him.

The Black Widow fell off as though the blow had poleaxed her.

"I've had it," Charley gasped over the line. "Let's get out
of here."

Green crawled toward the pilot, looked forward over his
shoulder, and saw the damage. There was a hole several inches

in diameter; shearing curved teeth of sheet metal back at a point directly above the front wheel mounting. That meant they'd never get that wheel down for a landing.

"You get it bad?" he asked Charley.

"Yeh, bad, maybe." Burke was struggling to get the Widow straightened out. She was corkscrewing down, screeching like a banshee through the hole in the snout, and the cold blast felt like an arctic drill boring in from under the instrument panel.

"What do you want to do—beat it?"

Charley considered that while he forced a wing tip down and eased her nose up. He turned and looked at Green.

"We—we can't go back yet. Look!"

Three sets of short flame sashes were curling around a short distance ahead of them. Green had seen them a few seconds before, and that meant some more transports would be getting it in a minute.

"Where you hit?"

"Low—legs. Take over, Lieutenant."

"But if you're hit bad . . ."

"You wanted to be a pilot, didn't you? What you waitin' for?"

"I'll try. You get back and patch yourself up."

Charley crawled from under the wheel, stopped, and gripped Green's elbow. "You're not going back, remember. You gotter make some sacrifice."

"You patch yourself up. I'll hang on somehow."

"We're responsible to those guys down there, remember."

Lieutenant Green slipped into Burke's seat and gripped the unfamiliar control. The bank of dials before him danced in frenzy. So this was command? He felt for the rudder pedals, and was mildly astonished to find that when he pressed one the Black Widow responded. He tried a timid bank and she answered with amazing docility. He tried it again, and gradually the dials settled back where they belonged. He could read them now.

Something lit a warm candle inside him and he glowed. *This* was command!

"Run 'em up to twenty-five hundred rpm!" he snarled at himself, and grinned. "Give 'em forty inches of boost. Make it five inches of supercharger instead of three. To hell with the gas gauge—and the fire balls!"

The engines joined his challenge as the Black Widow lunged forward.

"You all right, Burke?" he asked when he had jacked in his throat mike.

There was no answer. Burke hadn't hooked into the circuit behind. He looked back and saw his pilot hunched up on the floor, doing something with his knife. Probably slitting his pants. Green hoped he could keep warm.

The flame scarves were below now and racing for the black-ness behind. Green rolled the wheel over, depressed the rudder, and tore after them. He was amazed at the simplicity of it all. The Black Widow seemed to sing through her wound. She nosed down when he pushed the control forward. He could catch them in a matter of seconds.

Something tapped his arm. He turned to see Burke's pain-lined face. The wounded man was pointing up toward the back of the compartment.

"Use 'em all—top turret, too, Lieutenant."

"Of course. Thanks, Charley."

He pressed the action switch, confident now that the remote-control turret would swing and automatically aim its .50-caliber guns into position with the pilot's line of sight. He *knew* all that now. It was just a matter of command.

Charley huddled close to the base of Green's seat. "You're doin' all right, sir. Doin' all right."

"Sure! We're doing all right!"

The first burst hit a German wing man low, and he rolled over on his back and blew apart.

"You're doin' all ri—"

"All right? That's damn' near perfect!"

He depressed the right rudder and took aim again. The Widow

flounced her fanny twice, but eventually reconsidered and smoothed off—dead behind the second pair of exhaust streaks.

"Let 'em have it, Lieutenant! You're doin' all right."

The streams of fire from the Black Widow were as true as lines ruled in with scarlet ink. Green drew back gently on the control and hemstitched the Jerry neatly up the back.

"That won't do him a bit of good," Charley said quietly in the same tone he usually reserved for confession. "There he goes!"

Green nodded uncertainly and went after the third Jerry night fighter. He could see the twin slits of exhaust curling away for the east. He manipulated for more boost and went after him, but the Hun was too fast—in a steep dive.

"That's all you can do," Burke muttered. "That's the three of 'em. They won't bother our guys any more tonight. You just can't do any more, Lieutenant."

"Only get you back."

"That'll be funny. I hope—hope I see it. But maybe I won't."

"You're all right, aren't you?"

"I don't think you can get your front wheel down, sir. That means a two-wheel landing."

"Hang on, Charley. I'll get her where you can bail out—if you like."

"Sure, and freeze in some damn' swamp? I'm staying with you!"

"Don't worry. It won't be tough for me. I never set down a tricycle gear before, anyway."

"Swell! Just take her in—half flap—and keep your tail down. She'll go down on her nose soon enough for you, sir."

Lieutenant Green got her down with nothing much worse than a split lip. She skated along on her nose for a few yards, tossed her props away, and ground-looped hard. The landing didn't mark Charley....

The flight surgeon said they might have saved him if they had come straight in. But a guy loses a lot of blood hanging around, chasing Huns that way. Still, someone had to make a sacrifice. Burke probably wanted it that way. A guy can get a lot of funny ideas at night—up there.

Lieutenant Green didn't say anything. He just hoped they wouldn't try to kid *him* into becoming a pilot again. A guy has to make some sacrifices.

Merton of the Mustangs

SECOND LIEUTENANT MERTON UPDYKE Glassford, Mustang pilot of the 328th Fighter Squadron, had his initials stenciled on his B-bag; the stencil had not included periods, and the bare initials seemed to add up Merton's career with cruel conclusiveness. Merton was a mug from beginning to end. He was still a second lieutenant in spite of the fact that he had been in the service since Pearl Harbor. He had had his wings almost as long as Gabriel, but, unlike Gabriel, Merton never tooted his own horn. He seemed more willing to live up to his initials. He was a mug to everyone on the base; no officer of combat flying status ever won the Officer of the Day duty—except Merton. It seemed that there was no one in the A-to-G initials bracket lower than a captain, so Merton always caught the run-over ground-duty jobs. By that time the Equipment officer or the Photo Lab chief came back off pass, and the O.D. duty went back into the care of the paddlefeet.

Merton learned to fly with no more trouble than the average jerk, but ill-fortune dogged his hesitant footsteps. Somehow he missed shipping out with his own class from Sunnyfield because someone muffed giving him his full assortment of inoculations. By the time he did get overseas leave, he managed to contract a dose of the mumps—and missed out again. By this time there was a sudden demand for P-51 Mustang pilots, but Merton had graduated on P-38's, so back he went to Deedsville and took a conversion course on single-engined fighters. He wiped off three landing gears before he rediscovered how to put an orthodox two-wheeled ship back on the runway.

It was all very discouraging, but somewhere in Merton's skull an idea rattled which, when suitably warmed up, came out with the argument that if he could get one enemy plane, he would have paid for his keep. Merton was fair-minded that way.

Just one Jerry was all he craved. He was mulling it over one afternoon after he had reached Britain, and during this delicious mental lapse managed to smash three fingers while playing soft ball against the Headquarters crowd. This put the brake on his military career but resulted in his falling base over apex in love with Dolly Mulloy, the nurse attached to their field hospital.

Lieutenant Mulloy was removing Merton's splints and setting out the massage table when Merton brought this one-Hun business out into the open.

"I'm sorry to have given you all this trouble," he began.

"Trouble? It's no trouble," Dolly answered. "We've got to get this stiffness out. I guess the fingers on this hand are important in the air."

"They're important," Merton agreed with a wince. "That is, they will be if I can ever get upstairs and start shooting. It just seems ..."

"Never mind." Dolly smiled four bucks' worth of boost. "A few days of this, and we'll soon have you back in action."

"But I've never been in action!" Merton bleated. "It just seems—that is, every time I get to go, something always happens."

Lieutenant Mulloy looked up into his face and caught the wounded expression in his collie-brown eyes. For the first time she saw the pain of frustration that brought out the character of his shaggy aspect. It all came to her now. This was the boy who had edged up next to her that night the USO crowd had put on a show in the Officers' Club. She had been squired by Major Truscott, the latest rave in the Honors and Awards list, and she remembered, too, how Truscott had glared when this young second looie had somehow gleaned a few sentences of conversation.

"A friend of yours?" Truscott had growled.

"No. He just came and sat here."

"He's not annoying you, is he?" Truscott peered around her profile.

"Of course not. He—he just wanted to talk about the show, I guess. Don't you know him?" she had whispered.

"Yeh. He's in my squadron, but we can't seem to get him tuned up for combat."

"You see, I'm a jinx to myself," Merton was saying. "I arrive months late here in the E.T.O., and first crack out of the box, I bust my hand, just playing soft ball. Ouch!"

"Sorry. You're in Major Truscott's squadron, aren't you?"

Merton beamed. "I remember. You were with him at the USO show, weren't you? I guess he thinks I'm a weak sister. I've been here several weeks and I haven't even hit a contact mission yet."

"What's a contact mission?"

"Oh, you go out with the regular formation, but you don't go all the way; somewhere over the North Sea you turn back and fly up and down with your radio on, and you keep contact with the main formation. If anything unusual is reported, you relay it back here to the base. It's a job for lame ducks, or kids just getting started."

"But even that is important, isn't it?"

"I suppose so, but you don't get any shooting time in," Merton grumbled. "Golly, I'd like to get as hot as that Major Truscott. Ouch!"

"Am I hurting you?" Nurse Mulloy inquired with a smile.

"No. Your hands feel nice," Merton stammered. "I'm not saying anything I shouldn't, am I?"

"Of course not. But this must hurt some, at first. You're taking it pretty good. I guess you're tough—like that."

"Look, Lieutenant," Merton began again, with this sly encouragement, "I wouldn't be out of line if I asked you to help me celebrate some time—I mean, you and Major Truscott aren't engaged, or anything, are you?"

"You don't see a stoplight on my lily-white hand, do you? What's the celebration?"

"It's nothing immediate. You see, I sort of owe it to you—and all these people in the Air Corps—to pay for all the training and care they've given me."

"A celebration?"

"I mean, when I get my first German plane. I'd like to take you into Oxford and—well, celebrate."

"This will hurt some," she replied, taking one of his fingers in her hand and pulling gently.

"You mean you won't?" His face took on the expression of a foiled pelican.

"I didn't mean that. I was referring to this massage. What do you have in mind?"

"I thought we'd have dinner at Downing's and then take in a show. Those Garrison Players are pretty good."

"My, a stock company! That wouldn't be too steep, would it?" She smiled impishly. "Next finger."

"You're laughing at me." Merton almost pouted. "It's not funny to me. What I mean, I've got to get a Hun and square my account. By rights, I should get three, but I'll settle for one. What do you say?"

Lieutenant Mulloy eased her ministrations and looked into Merton's eyes. "You're really serious about this, aren't you?"

"A fellow has to have a goal in life," Lieutenant Glassford began again. A thin ray of hope tinted his horizon. "I mean, if you'd say you'd go with me—if I got a Jerry—it would mean a lot to me."

"I don't like the idea very much," Dolly Mulloy parried thoughtfully. "If anything happened, how do you think I'd feel? I'd never want to go to near Downing's again, or see the

Garrison Players. It would limit me to teashops and the movies."

Nurse Mulloy could have cut her tongue out the minute she said it. She knew it sounded brash and bitterly on the snide side and in no way reflected her true feelings. This freckle-nosed boy was getting under her skin. His was a new approach, and it was working. She hated herself for punishing him in this way, and she sought cover in her professional duties.

But the words never touched Merton. "Oh, don't worry about that, Lieutenant," he popped. "I'll be weeks even getting a contact assignment."

"Isn't there a chance you might meet enemy planes just doing a contact job? I mean, if you were all alone and were jumped by enemy planes?"

"Not a chance! Jerry is too busy these days protecting his own bases."

"Well, it's a date the day you get your first enemy plane, only don't go taking crazy chances. I'd hate to have anything happen to you *now*."

"Hey! Don't say it that way, Lieutenant. Golly, you look as though you were worried about me. It'll be . . ."

"I'm not worried about you!" Nurse Mulloy snapped suddenly. "Get out of here now, and come back the same time tomorrow. We'll have that fist in shape in no time."

Merton beamed in triumph. "It's a date, remember!"

"I sure hope so." Nurse Mulloy sniffed as the door closed.

The news of Merton's date spread through the base like wildfire. It came just when the gang needed a new topic of conversation.

Merton had no one but himself to blame for the chorus that shattered the usual quiet of dinner that night. So delighted had he been with the success of his venture that caution went to the four winds. He blurted it all out to his roommate, Kibby Kronkhite, before he realized what a nightmare could develop under Kibby's expert direction.

Kibby was one of those black-eyed little hellions whose curly hair crackled with his mischievous expectancy. He was short and knobby and had a capacity for needling equaled only by his ability to maintain the pressure.

This was manna from heaven for Kibby Kronkhite.

"Say that again!" he ordered from the end of his rumpled sack.

"Miss Mulloy, that is, Lieutenant Mulloy, the nurse, says she'll give me a date the day I get my first Hun. I just clinched it down at the sick bay."

"What size shoes do you wear?"

"What does that have to do with it?"

"I know your shirts won't fit, but what about your underwear? I guess I can get into that."

"I don't get it," Merton dithered.

"There's no use sending that sort of stuff home. I can use your gloves and scarf, and if you have any extra razor blades . . ."

Merton dropped to his bed and planted his mug between his hands. "Okay, Kibby. Lay off! I only asked her, and she said she would. A guy has to have some aim in life."

Kibby continued to pour it on. "Truscott will love that. He'll see you get a Hun. He'll let you have the first pack that comes up—all to yourself. Don't you know that Mulloy is Truscott's special dish?"

"I just asked her, that's all," Merton said tonelessly.

"That's all. All you have to do is get yourself a Hun, and Mulloy will give you a date. That's like asking you to walk through a prop. Well, it was nice knowing you. What about those shoes?"

"All right. You don't have to make a comedy out of it."

"Comedy? It's a tragedy! I mean, you going out to get a Jerry just to get a date with Mulloy! You don't get Huns that way, you dope! Guys don't get Huns until they've had weeks of experience. I've done fifteen combat missions, and I've hardly fired my guns yet. I suppose you want to go out tomorrow, just snorting for a Jerry formation."

"Truscott won't let me out for weeks yet. I'm willing to wait. This mitt will be some time loosening up."

"Sure! The major will have had three bachelor parties by then. He and Mulloy will be back home, the beaming service couple, selling bonds or kidding the war workers to assemble another Mustang."

"All right, Kibby. Just lay off. It was an idea."

"It's a beaut! Wait until the boys hear of this one."

From the purlieus of Lower Wallop-on-Tang a dank November fog crept across the field, and a drool of liquid murk drew a filter down Merton's window, blotting out a tableau staged outside the Officers' Club. Major Truscott was handing Lieutenant Mulloy into the colonel's staff car, obviously bent on an adventure in Oxford. Merton spent the rest of the afternoon running off Major Trustcott's combat film and studying just how to shoot down enemy fighters. Deep inside him Merton had an all-consuming respect for Major Truscott's ability to shoot down Me.-109's with his deadly deflection shots.

By dinner the full synopsis of Merton's beautiful pact with Mulloy had been explained to an enraptured audience by Kibby. Even the G.I. orderlies were interested, and when Lieutenant Glassford approached with his plate, Corporal Pukaski, who was officiating at the gravy tureen, inquired whether the lieutenant would have his beef raw or slightly underdone. "We've got to get you into shape, sir. You can lose a lot of blood, making those dates," Pukaski warned solicitously with the expression of a professional pallbearer.

Merton felt a large cold lump gathering below his breastbone. Kibby had started the spadework on the gigantic rib. The faces at the tables all bore the same mask of asinine inquiry.

"Hey, Merton!" Cobbie Slade yelled. "What'll you offer for a slightly damaged Focke-Wulf? I'll sell my share in it for your next week's cigarette ration."

"If she'll give you a date for one enemy fighter, what's the quotation on a Dornier bomber?" bellowed Skip Parker.

"But suppose he doesn't come back after he gets his Jerry." Bill Porter got to his feet and rapped for order with a tablespoon. "I suggest we get up a pool—just in case—and if Merton doesn't get back, the winner gets the date and the dough to entertain the lady."

"You can't tie up that much money that long," Captain Eggers, the public-relations officer, argued. "Merton won't be flying hate for weeks. He bruises so easily."

"No wonder the Germans want to scrap the Hague and Geneva conventions," Kibby tossed into the discussion. "Guys shooting down Jerries just to get a date with a broad. There's no telling where that sort of thing will end. It just ain't human."

Merton's eyes popped as he listened to Bill Porter's effort to form a pool on his chances, but he knew now how much that date meant to him, and the harangue only annealed his determination to wipe out at least half-a-dozen Luftwaffe squadrons to show his worth.

The next afternoon Merton had to report to Nurse Mulloy, after attending a lecture on the proper use of the escape hit. In the corridor Captain Carter, the flight surgeon, put his arm across Merton's shoulder and asked with pursed-lip gravity, "Let's see, was it Lancelot or Galahad who took on the Black Knight for a lady's garter? You'll find Lady Guinevere in the fracture ward."

Merton weathered that and strode on through a covered runway and listened as the Group took off, wondering when he'd get a chance to do a combat mission. He leaned over the rail and watched the blue-nosed Mustangs of Number 328 maneuvering into formation behind Major Truscott's gleaming P-51. He decided to go back and run those wing-camera films off again after he had passed through Nurse Mulloy's comforting hands.

"This way, Lieutenant," a voice called. "I'll take you in here."

It was Dolly Mulloy in a seersucker coverall of institution blue, but even this bleak garment could not erase her appealing lines. Dolly would have looked good in a diving suit to Merton, but he began to dither the minute he came close enough to interpret the accusation in her eyes.

"Nice going!" she began as she sat opposite him in the small physiotherapy room and started to remove the bandages. "You sure made a three-reeler comic out of it, didn't you?"

"I'm sorry. I—I didn't think. I just told Kibby Kronkhite, my roommate," explained Merton with a feeling that all controls had been shot away. "Everything's a big joke to that guy."

Nurse Mulloy didn't dare look at him. It was the tone of his voice and the way his hand trembled between her fingers. She began with a few of the loosening preliminaries, but winced when Merton recoiled with the pain.

"I suppose Major Truscott blew up," Merton ventured, but his mind wondered what she would look like in an evening gown at the country club back home. Something with little spangles on it. Not too much make-up, and a small red handkerchief in a bracelet at her wrist.

"Major Truscott has nothing to do with it." She wondered whether she should blow her nose. "I just don't care to have my private affairs discussed all over the base."

"But—but, Lieutenant," Merton gulped, "don't you see, I was so pepped up I just had to tell someone."

Dolly tried to get him off the subject, but she didn't want to smother the warm glow he seemed to bring into the room. "Captain Carter thinks we can leave these bandages off now, and you'd better start using these fingers a little. Do you play the piano?"

"I don't play anything, but I can exercise them putting film into the projector. I was doing it all yesterday afternoon, over at the pilots' room."

She looked up and tried to maintain her cool austerity, but the appeal in his eyes swept it away. She realized he needed more than her nursing care.

"I was running off Major Truscott's air-combat film," Merton continued to explain. "You can learn a lot that way. You know— the film his wing camera takes when he's bouncing a Jerry."

"That's—that's good for your fingers?" she asked, puzzled.

"Of course. Threading that film through those intricate sprockets and rollers is good exercise, I'd say."

"And you run the film off, too—after you thread them in?"

"Sure. The major's really hot. It's just like being in the cockpit with him. It's the best sort of training, really." Merton's words were torrenting out like the .50-caliber slugs from Truscott's guns.

"You're still aiming to get that Hun, aren't you? I guess I started something." She smiled.

A hopeful light flashed in Merton's eyes. "You mean the date's still on, Lieutenant?"

"In spite of what Kibby Kronkhite says," she assured him. "Now let's try this other finger. . . ."

The 328th had a bad day, covering the Forts and Libs on a Leipzig mission, and the Mustangs were down all over the place. A few were safe somewhere outside Brussels, and two crash-landed at Manston on the southeast coast. Three pilots of the Group were being treated at the field hospital for flak wounds, and by nightfall the whole base was alerted and the station closed.

In the reception hall of the Officers' Club Merton caught up with Major Truscott who was pinning up a notice. He turned when Merton squinted around his shoulder and tried to read it.

"Ho! I've been wondering about you," Truscott boomed. "How's your hand?"

"Coming along fine, sir." Merton flexed his fingers experimentally.

"Not too good, but keep at them," Truscott said as though he had never heard of the Mulloy-Glassford pact. "I'll need all the

men I can get my hands on in the next few days. You're in
reserve and will probably get the radio-contact assignment with
young Chambers. I want you to take it seriously, because you
can get bounced. Jerry has a lot of stuff over this way, trying to
check on the V-2 hate he's been throwing over. Hit the sack
early; you may fly tomorrow!"

"Thank you, sir," Merton breathed, overwhelmed with the
honor. "I'll be on hand." He hoped Nurse Mulloy wouldn't be
too busy with the wounded to make that trip into Oxford....

Merton caught himself whistling as he dressed for dinner.

"What are you so gay about?" Kibby demanded. "We get a
pasting, and you come up with 'Hark, the Herald Angels Sing.'"

"Major Truscott has me on the alert list. Maybe only for a
radio contact, but you can't tell."

"What about those fingers?"

"Coming along swell. Another treatment today just about
did it," Merton explained, playing an imaginary Steinway.

"Wait until you hit twenty-five thousand feet and see what
the cold does to them," Kibby warned. "Still, just on radio
contact you probably won't get into too much trouble."

"You can't tell. A Jerry might be out in that area, snooping
around. I might get a pass at one."

"Look!" Kibby said, and sat up straighter. "You're not still
on that Mulloy quest?"

"She says it's still on. I can't let her down now."

"Merton, if you'd seen what we saw today, you'd play that mitt
of yours up for another month. Ann Sheridan or Lana Turner
wouldn't get me into the air right now—if I could get out of it."

"Was it that bad?"

"I was scared—plenty scared." Kibby groaned.

"Did they have many fighters up?"

"Fighters, flak, rockets, and everything came up. The flak was
bad, but Jerry was up there fighting today. He's a tough apple
when he wants to fight. I can't picture you..."

"The trick," Merton explained, taking over and making

one hand shoot flat passes at the other, "is to make him turn to
the right. All Jerry fighters are slow in right-hand turns. Maybe
they overcontrol and get into a sideslip. You figure for that and
you'll get strikes on him every time."

Kibby cupped his hands over his knees, cocked his head side-
wise, and exploded: "What the hell you been reading now—all
this handies business?"

"Listen, Kibby. I've been running Major Truscott's combat
film off, and I have it all figured out. The 190, in particular, really
sideslips in a right-hand turn, and you have to allow for it. I ran
off about a dozen of them."

"Sure! You ran off the ones that show Truscott shooting down
something. What about the times he fired and Jerry got away?
They don't let us see those, remember."

"No. They don't show us the misses, do they?" Merton agreed
thoughtfully. "I wonder if they all sideslip."

"Don't bet on anything in this war," advised Kibby. "Not
even on a date. As the RAF guys say, you can come unstuck."

After hours of painful delay Merton received the Call three
mornings later. He was briefed with the rest and given his
escape kit, and he tucked away the various packages so neces-
sary for the successful aerial adventure. Everyone smiled at him;
some of the flight leaders slapped him on the back and said kind
words. He was certain Colonel Ralston was looking directly at
him when he presented the details of enemy-fighter concentra-
tions. There were minutes when Merton was certain he could
have taken on half-a-dozen Me.-109's and shot them apart to the
tune of "The Skaters' Waltz." As a matter of fact, he was
whistling Waldteufel's old classic as he started out.

"You getting that Hun today, Merton?" Skip Parker inquired
as they climbed into the truck.

"You can't tell. I'm doing radio contact today with Chambers."
Merton grinned. "A guy has to work up."

"Sure, you can shoot each other down if it gets dreary," Bill Clark added with a moody grimace.

"Didn't you have to do a couple of radio contacts before you went over?"

"How can a guy remember that far back?" Bill wheezed.

"I'm perfectly satisfied," Merton said from the fullness of his heart. "We might get bounced, even doing a contact mission."

"Sure! Some of those sea gulls aren't to be trusted," Clarkie ribbed.

"Let's go!"

"Wait a minute. Here's Colonel Lawrence. Now what?"

The Group Operations officer came out to the tailboard of the truck with a small strip of paper in his hand.

"Is Glassford in there? . . . That you, Glassford? You're flying radio contact, aren't you?" he called up over the tailboard.

"Yes, sir. Lieutenant Chambers and I," Merton peeped.

"Well, wash that out. There's a kite balloon loose, heading northeast out of one of the restricted areas the other side of Whitney. The damn thing's dragging a length of steel cable cross country and doing a lot of damage. Short-circuited a main hydro-electric system already. You take off at once and take care of it. Last seen heading northeast out of Bicester. Chambers can do the radio contact. You get that balloon. Shoot it down!" Colonel Lawrence handed Merton the slip of paper and waved the truck away.

Merton sat down with the expression of a man trying to swallow a doorknob. "I'm—I'm not going with you," he finally gasped, although all of them had heard the colonel's orders. "I—I've got to go and shoot down a balloon."

The whole truckload of pilots was still in a paroxysm of delight when Merton clambered over the tailboard and headed for his Mustang.

"Three to one the balloon knocks down Merton!" Porter yelled.

Glassford had no Mustang of his own. He had been assigned

to fly Captain Montgomery's, which sported no less than seventeen black swastika victory insignia painted under the cockpit canopy track. The captain was away on leave, and his ground crew greeted Merton's approach with slabs of black doubt.

"You flying the captain's ship, Lieutenant?" Staff Sergeant Gillsum asked, trying his best to stifle his horror.

"That's right. But don't worry, I'm only going up to knock down a runaway kite balloon." Merton selected his words carefully. "I was to do a radio contact, but..." He climbed up and jabbed savagely at the starter. The big prop semaphored, the exhaust spat, gulped, and finally the engine broke into a thunderous roar. Merton slipped the sheet of instructions under a map prong and called the tower.

"Blue Five calling Galaxy ... Blue Five calling Galaxy. All set for special assignment. Are you receiving me?"

"Get going, Glassford," the colonel answered from the tower, ignoring the niceties of field communication. *"Get going, or you'll be cluttering up the runway assembly."*

"He couldn't even give me an official send-off," Merton muttered bitterly as he ran the Mustang around the perimeter track and swung into the number-three runway. "At least I had that coming to me."

The balloon, which had been one of a special group that had been sent to protect a sprawling aircraft engine factory in the Midlands, had once sat majestically above the fringes of Hyde Park. It had reigned for months in bulbous defense of London's Mayfair, but with the coming of Jerry's buzz bombs, shortly after D-Day, *Fat Anna*, as the WAAF ground crew had christened her, was hurriedly and with scant ceremony deflated and trucked off to a bleak industrial district.

Fat Anna showed her displeasure from the start. Soon after she had been inflated and sent up for a preliminary look around she developed valve trouble. What she saw needled her pride and, dowager duchess that she was, she immediately settled back to earth again at an unwarranted rate of descent. Next she fouled her instrument tackle and smashed up some very hush-hush meteorological equipment. A gruff flight sergeant appeared and gave *Fat Anna* a rare going over, and for a few weeks all seemed secure and serene. The pay-off came, after this period of relative calm, when *Fat Anna* somehow fouled her cable in the winch, and before the ground crew could reel back, the big balloon had snapped it off and went floundering away in the general direction of northwestern Germany, dragging three thousand feet of steel cable with her.

In her wake *Fat Anna* left a trail of damaged Georgian chimneypots, overturned war memorials of the Crimean era, short-circuited a vast expanse of high power lines, and left dozens of outraged housewives speechless as they watched their clothes-lines go dragging through acres of tar-papered Victory Garden sheds, with no visible means of propulsion.

It requires little imagination to understand *Fat Anna's* feelings or her mission; but what perverse artifice of fate sent Merton out to put an end to her unlawful adventures? After all, Merton and *Fat Anna* had much in common.

As the tepid sun of early morning gradually marshaled its thermals, the unseasonable warmth expanded the power within *Fat Anna's* bosom, and the old girl joyfully zoomed for higher altitude.

It was here amid the sun-gilded halls of space that *Fat Anna* made her great mistake, for Merton spotted her through a massed garden of formal clouds heading toward the coast of Lincolnshire, materially assisted by a spanking tail wind. He circled her twice to make certain she was on the loose. He kept clear of the trailing cable, but followed it down until he was positive it was not connected with anything of an official nature below.

"That's her," he finally deduced, and started back aloft to finish her off. "I could use this old bag to practice some of that

Truscott business. Let's see, he makes a fake pass this way—to the left, which makes Jerry nose around to the right. Then . . ."

Something went *Bong! Bong! Bong!* above and ahead of *Fat Anna*. Merton leaped against his safety belt and forgot about Major Truscott's deadly maneuvers. No question about it, someone was shooting at the balloon!

"All right! All right! You needn't get your backs up. I'll shoot it down!"

There were three big blossoms of smoke just ahead now, and Merton circled the balloon again, figuring a British ack-ack battery below was getting impatient.

"If you guys wanted to shoot it down, why didn't you say so?" Merton asked without bothering to cut in his transmitter switch. "I could have gone on that mission then."

He banked sharply, and decided to put over the old one-two from one of Major Truscott's famous dives and come up and under the gas bag. "That gets Jerry in his blind spot," he recited as he set his sight. "I ought to be . . ."

Bong! Bong! Bong!

Three more ordnance orchids blossomed out, and Merton held off and wondered why they hadn't turned the balloon over to the antiaircraft crowd before. Then it dawned on him that to destroy it at close range with machine-gun fire was much safer than filling the sky with three-pounder shell casing, nose caps, and chunks of sharp rotation bands. Still, if they were shooting at the balloon, they were putting on a pretty soggy show. They weren't even close yet.

"All right! All right! I'll show you how to get it. Just hold your horses!"

He nosed down and rushed at the balloon, which was now slithering for a serried bank of cloud. He held her steady in spite of the increased ack-ack fire that raged all about him. Then he brought the stick back smoothly and set the rigging web of the bag well inside the reflector sight. He pressed the gun releases and streams of .50-caliber slugs tore *Fat Anna* to shreds. With a quick forward flip of the stick, Merton shot under the inflated rudder bag to avoid the trailing cable and tackle, and then felt sixteen triphammers beating an ear-splitting tattoo on his port wing.

"Hey! What the—" he began, but the metallic drumming suddenly ceased. As Merton banked again, he heard a muffled explosion. Turning in his cockpit, two undeniable panels of evidence caught his eye.

First: *Fat Anna*, painfully misshapen and ablaze at her grommet lacings, actually winked a cocarded eye; it was a very smug and self-satisfied wink.

Next: To Merton's astonishment, a Jerry F.W.-190 fighter charged out of the blazing tangle of the balloon, fouled itself with *Fat Anna's* cable, and screwed around wildly like a paper canary on a string. There wasn't any question of its being a Jerry, and Merton realized immediately what the ack-ack batteries had been firing at. He sensed, too, that the Focke-Wulf had followed him down when he went at the balloon, but had zoomed and turned the wrong way, and had hit the trailing steel cable that Merton had so carefully avoided.

"There's my Jerry!" he gulped, and whipped over fast. "That guy was tailing me all the way down. Why, the . . ."

Merton's Mustang went at the cable-entangled Focke-Wulf with everything wide open. *Fat Anna* winked the other eye as the flames engulfed her, but Merton was thinking of Dolly Mulloy as he shot the Jerry to pieces.

"There won't be any argument about that," Merton decided. "Maybe he hit the cable, but he'll have enough of my ammo in to satisfy—even Major Truscott. Golly, I hope that wing camera was operating. What a reel! What a picture!"

"Well, was it worth it, Merton?" Nurse Mulloy asked that night in the darkness of the Garrison Players theater.

"Worth it? Listen, Lieutenant—I mean Dolly," he whispered. "I don't care if they give Captain Montgomery credit for it. He can even paint another Jerry victory on his ship, but they can't take this away from me." And he gripped her hand even tighter.

Pip, Squeak, and Wilfred

THE alert room didn't appear particularly alert. It was long and low and had all the characteristics of a disused rabbit warren. The lights were dim and the battered tin stove smoked.

"If Grimes hadn't been so cocky about Beaufighters being better than Hurricanes, it wouldn't have happened," the skipper of Red Flight, Morse, grumbled from behind the goggles that shielded his eyes.

"Well, they are better, aren't they?" demanded old Jackson, the Air Intelligence officer. "I mean to say, you chaps have *two* engines. Now in the last war we were flying Bristol Fighters..."

Splinter Dingley took it up from there. Splinter was young enough to appreciate Jackson. The other war still retained a certain aura of individual crusade, whereas night flying with Number 112, RCAF, was too cut and dried.

"It's like this, Jackson," Splinter began. "Just before you came, Squadron Leader Grimes was awarded the D.S.O. There was a blowout of some sort at a pub in Peterborough and Grimes made a bet with Brannix of Number 86. They're a Hurricane crowd."

Old Jackson nodded and folded his fingers over his belt buckle. He was a pudgy old gaffer who persisted in wearing a gorblimey cap, even though he had a face that only could have flattered a Beefeater's bonnet. Beneath his fuzzy observer's wing were three drab campaign ribbons earned a quarter of a century before.

Pip, Squeak, and Wilfred, the Canadian Beaufighter boys had dubbed them.

"Anyway," Splinter went on, "old Grimes made a goofy bet before he bowed out that night. He put up our Moocher as a prize for the outfit that wrapped up the most Jerries every month."

"The Moocher?" Old Jackson pursed his lips and frowned thoughtfully at the battered stove.

"Also before your time here," young Dingley explained further. "The Moocher was our furlough service bus. A real slick bit of equipment. Used to be a Trans-Dominion Airlines courtesy car that took passengers from the Royal Tudor in Toronto out to the airport. Grimes pinched it one night and tooled it all the way to Halifax and somehow got it aboard a transport. Now 86 has it because they nudged us out last month in Jerry kills and look like they'll be doing it again. If we get a forty-eighter or a spot of leave now we have to go out to the station in one of those poisonous service lorries."

"Hardly dignified, considering everything," old Jackson pronounced. "Beaufighters ought to be better—two engines."

"What does that have to do with it?" Flight Lieutenant Morse ranted. "The Control girls seem to shove all the trade the Hurricanes' way."

"Are those WAAF girls allowed to wear silk stockings?" Dean Warburton, the third member of Red Flight, inquired, as he sat up suddenly. He had been lolling back with his feet high on the back of a chair. His mat of crisp curly hair topped off a long, aristocratic face; and he, too, wore black glasses to contract the pupils of his eyes before flying at night.

Morse studied Warburton's question for a minute and then ignored it. "You're the Intelligence bloke in this mob," he thundered at Jackson. "Why don't you do something about getting us some work upstairs, instead of bending everyone's ear with your yarns about the other war? You Pip, Squeak, and Wilfred guys!"

"But I don't quite see ..." Jackson tugged at his face fungus.

Morse blundered on. "Over at Number 86 they have Intelligence birds who are gay young blades. Screwballs, maybe, but they managed to grab the inside track with the WAAF's at the radio-locator station. What's the answer?"

"They probably have the straight on the accessories business," broke in Warburton. "Stockings and stuff. Looks like that's your cue, Jackson."

"If that's what you're dealing me in for, sounds a bit out of my line." Jackson produced a gloomy grimace. "Still, perhaps I can manage it. I'd like to see you chaps get that transport back."

The crisp chatter of battle reports was coming in from a loud-speaker on the wall. There was a Hurricane flight upstairs somewhere, demanding a bit of business from the Control operators.

"Ginger patrol to Salisbury," an English flight lieutenant was reporting. "Come on, Gladys. All we need is a couple more."

Morse almost choked as he pointed up at the speaker. "He means our Moocher. Those guys must have sisters in the WAAF!"

A steady, well-modulated feminine voice answered the Hurricane skipper. "Attention, Ginger patrol. Salisbury to Ginger. Three bandits.... Angels seven, approaching Felixstowe. Area 13-9.... Area 13-9.... Over to you!"

The Hurricane skipper answered back with gloating in his voice. "Ginger to Salisbury.... Bandits three.... Angels seven. Thank you, Gladys. Are you receiving me? ... Over."

"Signal clear ... about nineish.... Take it, Ginger patrol."

Morse picked at an imaginary wisp of straw between his teeth. "Those guys have the luck of a wart hog. They've been out of their area for forty minutes, skidding about at eleven thousand. Now they get three sitters coming in at seven thousand. All they have to do is stick their noses down and press the button."

"Whammo! There goes our furlough bus for another month," Splinter prattled.

From across the room the sergeant gunners looked up expectantly for another juicy bit from Warburton. They were expressionless figures and seemed to be turned out of the same mold. They wore the same oil-stained trousers, the same short flying boots. All semblance of personality and character was blotted out by the owlish black glasses that shielded their eyes.

Old Jackson looked up accusingly at the loud-speaker. "That's what's wrong with *this* war," he exploded with a grotesque attempt at posturing. "Blasted mess is too—too organized. Everything's done to a formula. It's got to where a lot of long-legged girls run the show from a switchboard. Where's there a chance for any individuality—like in the last war?"

"Here he goes again," Morse moaned.

"By George! You should have seen our Major Murdock and how he got his D.S.O. Chased a Hun triplane down the Street of the Three Pebbles wearing nothing more than his pajamas and a silk hat. He got the Hun and piled him up on some church steps. I don't know where he got the silk hat."

"Standard equipment in those days," Warburton chimed in. "Silk hats and maternity jackets."

"I'll bet they did have fun in the last war," young Dingley agreed.

"No individuality in this go," Jackson grumbled. "All done by a lot of girls at a switchboard. Good lord! You even have parachutes. A war run by a lot of girls."

The loud-speaker agreed with another rasp of its vibrator plates. "Ginger patrol to Salisbury. Ginger to Salisbury. Attacked two Dorniers. One in flames over Harwich. One probable—scuttled off in the murk. Will you confirm with Observer Corps, please? Over!"

"Salisbury to Ginger patrol. One Dornier confirmed. Area 13-9 . . . 13-9. Return to base and pancake. Over."

"Ginger patrol. Ginger to Salisbury. Give us fifteen minutes more, please. Wish to—"

"Sorry. Return to base. Ginger patrol, pancake. Over."

"Righto! Ginger to Salisbury. Patrol returning, and will old Morsie of 112 be hopping!"

The Control operator chided the flight lieutenant for irrelevant wordage as Morse stood wide-legged before the loud-speaker. "Why, you pawnbroker's striker, you! Picking on old Dorniers. Tumbleweeds! We get nothing but Focke-Wulfs." Morse was blazing. He spun on his heel and charged at the Intelligence officer.

"Look here, Jackson. How about rustling us some business? There's only one night to go, you know."

The pudgy bloke stood up and pulled down his tunic. "I'll see what I can do. I can't put Dorniers up there, you know. The devils have to come over, and those Hurry-up chaps can't get them all."

He hesitated outside the gleam of the lamp and peered over at the gunners. He squinted at them, one by one, and then waddled out muttering something indistinguishable.

Morse paced the length of the Nissen hut. His ear was cocked for the loud-speaker, but his mind weighed the remaining time brackets of the competition. He felt the ignominy of their having to use a service lorry when they could have luxuriated triumphantly in their own airline bus. On the surface it was ridiculous, but he argued with himself that there had to be some standards and as skipper of Red Flight he had done very little to improve their score. Whether it was D.F.C.'s, Huns, or lorries, one had to have a goal.

Warburton studied him pensively and then suddenly erupted: "I wonder what size silk stockings a long-legged girl wears."

The gunners took interest again and grinned.

Morse interrupted his pacing. "Just what is this?"

"Well, I mean to say, most of these radio-locator wenches at Control are a bit on the lanky side. I asked a girl in a teashop the other day about it, but she just slapped my face."

Morse threatened to explode, but Warburton explained: "I only asked her if she wore silk—and what size."

"You haven't stopped a splinter lately?" Morse asked solicitously. "A bit of flak somewhere?"

"You wouldn't understand. Anyway, it's up to my brother now
—in Montreal."

The gunners in the shadows rustled and assumed their bored
expressions. It was obvious that Warburton was off on another
of his pointless discussions. They got up, moved about, and
flexed their arms and legs as they considered the possibility of
getting off the ground that night.

A sleepy-eyed corporal opened the door, came in, and saluted.
"They want Sergeant Bull over at the adjutant's office, sir."

"Bull? What's the flap now?"

"I wouldn't know, sir."

"Don't tell me leave is starting again," Warburton suggested
cheerfully.

"Don't keep him long," Morse warned.

"They've probably been censoring the letters again. I'm always
putting my foot in it," Bull commented with a smirk from the
doorway.

"If it's leave," Splinter called, "have 'em hold it off for a
day or two. We've got to get the Moocher back."

Sergeant Gunner Bull waved uncertainly from the door.

"I think they're giving Bull a transfer," Morse explained with
a worried look. "No sooner do we get a chap lined up so he's
some use to us than they take him away."

They sat and chivvied the subject for several minutes and
came to the decision that gunners aboard Beaufighters were not
getting the best of the deal. It was agreed that they were
gunners in that they loaded the fixed guns for the pilots—
actually, they were only radio operators. They had no guns
of their own.

The loud-speaker broke up the academic discussion with: "Red
Flight . . . At Readiness!"

That came from the squadron Intelligence room. Evidently old

Jackson had flushed up something. The speaker cranged, cleared its throat, and added: At Super-Readiness! Red Flight... at Super-Readiness!"

"That's us," Morse thundered, and grabbed for his equipment. "On your way, boys."

The two remaining gunners were ready first. They twisted the air cocks of their Mae Wests, gave them a couple of puffs to make certain the valves were clear, and listened to the air wheeze out. As they clumped toward the door the loud-speaker announced: "Formation of Focke-Wulfs sitting over the Channel off Margate. Bandits waiting for squadron of American Fortresses on their way back from Amiens.... Red Flight at Super-Readiness."

"Good old Amiens," Warburton cackled. "I remember somewhere there in 1743 we captured the standard of the Black Musketeers of France. I think we were mercenaries then."

"What the heck are we now?" Morse pushed him toward the door. "Besides, that was the First Dragoon Guards and it all happened at Dettingen."

"Good lord! We must be older than Jackson."

"Where the devil is Bull?" Splinter Dingley said suddenly.

"Don't worry. He'll be out at the dispersal bay. Shove off!" Morse barked. "Remember, we're Gibbon patrol tonight."

"I'll be a monkey's uncle," Warburton announced.

They raced out to the dispersal area and the wail of Tannoy speakers joined the snarl of starting engines. Dim figures darted about and flashed through the shadows of a Hollis fuel lorry as a flight sergeant bellowed orders against the tympany of the night.

The glowering Beaufighters huddled in their bays—great animals restrained in their stanchions, below their bellies shovel-shaped doors hung like armored udders. Pilots and gunners scrambled up the rungs bolted to the inside of the doors, disappeared, and slammed the panels after them.

Young Dingley, sconced with a massive service helmet, peered

through a side window of his cockpit. He called down to the
flight sergeant and inquired about Bull.

"He's coming now, sir."

"Good! Rush him along, will you?"

Splinter turned down the cockpit lights, adjusted his Sutton
straps, and made certain his harness safety pin was in position.
He listened while Morse talked it over with Control and reported: "Red Flight I . . . Gibbon patrol to Salisbury. Ready to
take off . . . Over to you."

"Red 3 calling," Splinter broke in. "Just a minute—I need a
gunner."

They waited a few seconds and Splinter saw the flight sergeant hurrying someone toward the belly hatch. The gunner disappeared and Splinter felt the hatch close with a clang.

"Red 3 to Red 1 . . . All clear. Ready, Red 1." He spoke into
his flap mike.

Operations was chattering a new sheaf of data and then gave
a course. Splinter Dingley scribbled it on his thigh pad and
listened again. Aft, his gunner was setting out his stall, banging
down the navigation table, plugging in his headphone jack and
oxygen supply.

"All clear here, sir," the gunner reported over the intercom.

"Right. Thought you would miss the bus. What happened?"

"Nothing much, sir," the voice from the compartment aft
responded.

"Good! Batten down for take-off."

Morse ran his Beaufighter out and turned her around at the end
of the flare path. The others followed, rumbling and creaking
over the packed runway. They got the green light triggered
from an Aldis lamp on the control lorry hatch, and listened
while Morse checked his signal strength.

Together they thundered away into the sable night.

A gentle right-hand turn at one thousand feet put them dead

on their course and they slipped into open formation, snapped off their navigation lights, and headed for the coast.

Splinter Dingley reveled in his post off the starboard wing of his flight leader. He'd been with Number 112 for seven weeks now. They had worked him in carefully and the effort had produced a true reward. He was temperamentally suited for twin-engine machines and had a touch for engine synchronization that is not always acquired—even by the best. But even more important was the fact that he was a natural night-flying pilot.

Sergeant Bull swore he had cat's eyes.

"Gibbon patrol to Salisbury," Morse began again. "Gibbon to Salisbury. Angels twelve over B-area 19-6. . . . Over to you."

The voice in the Control room tucked away in Salcey Forest responded with: "Salisbury to Gibbon patrol. Ten-plus bandits patrolling northeast of Le Havre. . . . Angels fourteen . . . Over."

Splinter listened intently as Morse responded and repeated the information. The youngster grinned at the bank of glowing instruments and hoped they would get some trade this time. The gunners would be marking the position on their charts, and, by rights, Bull should be moving forward to check the ammunition drums fitted to the four cannon tucked away under the pilot's cockpit.

Two deep lines apexed a frown above Splinter's nose. His tongue felt thick and seemed to stick to the roof of his mouth. He sensed that the normal routine aboard the night fighter was skewwhiff. Bull was not reporting through; the old bustling efficiency was missing. Instead, there was cringing letdown in the schedule. The silence and inaction were as apparent as an off-pitch propeller.

"What about it, Bull?" he blustered over the intercom.

"Yes, sir. What is it?" a voice came back.

"Don't I get a report tonight? What about the plumbing?"

There was no answer, and Splinter twisted in his seat to look over the low bulkhead that separated his seat from the radio-navigation compartment. Bull was huddled up over the naviga-

tion table, an indistinct figure in his helmet, Mae West, and tunic
from which gleamed his rank stripes. The adjustable light brought
out certain unfamiliar details. Bull should have been wearing a
flying jacket—it would be getting cold any minute. Splinter
wondered if he felt all right. He checked his position again and
listened as the engines took on the new decibel note that always
came when they were over the waters of the Channel.

"Hey! Come up here, Bull. Are you all right?" he inquired.

He checked Warburton's position and watched Morse's wing
tip until the gunner appeared around the bulkhead. There was
plenty of flak ahead and the young pilot realized they were heading into action of some sort. Morse's voice trumpeted over the
set again and Splinter noticed that the leader was wagging his
wings as an alert signal. "Keep buttoned up, you guys," Morse
added stiffly. "There's our assignment up front."

Splinter was waiting for Bull to report when Warburton
chimed in. "That's more than flak, Skipper. That's our leave bus.
All we have to do is—"

"Bull!" Splinter yelled. "What about it? I want a report on
my guns."

"It's not Bull," a voice answered from behind his shoulder.
"Bull was busy, so I borrowed his tunic and came aboard in
his place."

Splinter wrenched around as though he had been jabbed with
a commando dirk. Old Jackson stood beside him—old Jackson,
a caricature of an airman in a helmet several sizes too small that
carried a set of earphones as big as custard pots. He beamed
pleadingly over the chin piece.

"What the deuce are *you* doing here?" Splinter finally bawled.

"I came along as radio operator—and I thought I could help
out from the rear turret." Old Jackson stared about. "I did so
want to go on patrol again, but I clean forgot about the guns—
that we don't carry a gunner's turret on this kite."

"Where's Bull?" Splinter demanded.

"He was busy signing some papers and having a medical. He's

getting a commission and going back to Canada to train for a pilot. He had to have an examination for his embarkation papers, so I saw my chance, picked up his tunic and helmet, and got by the flight sergeant. But now I remember there's no gun turret for me."

"Never mind that. Can you load the guns? That's the gunner's job aboard this bus."

"No—I'm afraid not. I've never had the opportunity. Still, if there's anything else..."

"There isn't. There are four guns below, and they carry ammo drums that have to be changed when they're empty. That means we can stay in action about three minutes at the most."

"I'm sorry, but we'll have to do the best we can," Jackson encouraged with a faint smile. "After all, three minutes is something. If I hadn't come, you'd have had to remain on the ground. Bull wouldn't have been available for some time."

There was no argument to that, so Splinter sent him back to the dorsal hatch and ordered him to keep a stiff watch on their tail.

"Three minutes," Splinter grumbled, "and we need at least four Jerries."

Morse gave them orders again as the three Beaufighters nosed down slightly and pumped after the business up ahead. "Trundle in, Gibbon patrol," he snapped. "We'll get the Moocher back yet. Ten-plus, they said. Looks more like dozens to me."

Splinter swallowed hard and thumbed the safety collar off the gun button on his wheel. He reached forward, twisted the knob of the reflector sight, set it for a wing span of about forty feet, and dimmed it slightly. A stile of searchlight beams unfolded from below and began waving its elements back and forth. The Channel was as clear as a design embossed on bright pewter. He wondered about Dieppe and what would happen if he force-landed there with "Canada" embroidered on his sleeve. The searchlight blades crisscrossed as if to hone their edges.

Morse was raging again. "Just our blasted luck!" he yelled.

Splinter squinted as he tried to make it all out. There was plenty of tracer and strings of sparkling ping-pong balls bouncing into the sky. There were splintered streaks that snapped off at right angles, lobbed into lazy trajectories, and spluttered off into nothing.

"What's wrong Skipper?" Warburton asked.

"Don't you see? They're Yank Fortresses nailing down *our* Focke-Wulfs. Look at them! They're having a picnic!"

"We'd better stay away, then. Those Fortress guys may go gun crazy, if they have any luck, and take a smack at anything."

"Nothing doing! I'm having a whirl at it. We'll never get a chance like this. We can slither through a searchlight, show our markings, and yell, 'Shinny on your own side!' They'll understand that line."

Flight Lieutenant Morse took them in and sought a Focke-Wulf. He rammed boldly through a searchlight blade to show his night-fighter markings and then yelled into his flap mike, "Three Beaufighters here. Three Canucks, you guys. Don't waste any on us!" He hoped the Americans were tuned into his Control wave length.

Splinter was figuring all the way in; he had one pan available in each gun, which meant that he might be able to stay in the action for several minutes if he conserved his bursts—and had a lot of luck. Figures danced before him and he suddenly realized that it was well past midnight—that it was already Saturday, and that by the time they'd be in the air again, a new month would have begun. They had to get at least four Jerries on this show to nudge out the Hurricane crowd. He wondered if Morse realized it, too, so he called Red 1 and explained.

"Don't I know it!" Morse replied. "Four tonight—or nothing. Let's go!"

Young Dingley spotted something dark and ominous with a big radial engine cowling. "Watch out for our tail, Jackson," he called over the intercom as he swung over after a Focke-Wulf that was charging into a Fortress. The glare from exhaust ports and the reflected sheen from the searchlight broadswords plated the sides of the contesting machines and brought out the recognition details. Splinter sat and took the pressure, while quaking deep in his heart in the fear that he'd pile into something not so distinct. Another searchlight slashed between him and his target and for a minute he lost it. He curled over, his prop tips screaming, and shot out into the full glare of a 190 that was banking sharply at him.

"Hang on to your medals, Jackson," he called, and pressed the button.

The heavy-caliber guns raged in the gallery below, four streaks of metallic blasphemy shot across the sky and buried their fangs in the fuselage of the Focke-Wulf. The German fighter zoomed as though she had been gaffed. Splinter leveled off, moved into position below and behind, and waited for the stall. The Nazi fighter writhed in agony, gushed two serpents of flame from the wing root, and fell off.

With his eyes still glued on the doomed Focke-Wulf, Splinter banked gently and watched her spin. He S-turned twice and timed his final bank so his nose would be on the fighter when she showed the top of her cockpit.

"Red 2 to Red 1," Warburton was calling across the night sky. "Red 2 to 1 . . . Credit us with one . . . but Consequences . . . Consequences, Red 1."

There was a second to think. That meant Warburton had knocked down one somewhere—but the Consequences indicated he was clearing off with a wounded crew member. It could be Warburton himself, or Wells, his gunner.

The cockpit top Splinter had been waiting for appeared. He let fly with a burst that cut the tumbling Focke-Wulf in two.

"Red 3 to Red 1 . . . Red 3 to Red 1," he reported as he cleared. "One bandit down . . . one bandit down . . . a flamer!"

Still no answer from Morse. Splinter hoped the skipper was all right—there was plenty of wreckage in the air.

"You all right, Jackson?" he inquired.

"Righto, Splinter. How're we doing?"

"Warburton got one but he's clearing off. Either he or Wells has stopped something. I can't raise Morse. . . . Hello! Just a minute."

"Red 1 to Red 3 . . . Red 1 to Red 3," Morse finally came through. "Keep after them, Splinter. We have three now. I poleaxed one, but I spent all I had on the swine. Hang on somehow. We need another."

Splinter frowned again as he tooled the black Beaufighter through the melee and shot across a stepped-up echelon of American bombers. That meant Morse had expended his ammunition and was through.

Another Focke-Wulf shot through a silver picket and flashed his markings. The gunners aboard the Fortresses tried to get at him, but they were out of range now. Splinter looked around and sensed that the last Nazi fighter was chucking it.

"It's a chance," he admitted, and tore after it. "Watch my tail, Jackson. I'm going after that one."

"How're we doing?"

"We need one more. Here's hoping."

The Focke-Wulf appeared again against the tumbling blaze of a falling plane. Splinter sucked in his breath, stiffened with the pressure, and brought his nose dead on.

"I've got to get him with what I have left, and I can't have much. I gave the other guy two long bursts."

The heavy Beaufighter was on the fleeing Focke-Wulf in a few seconds. Splinter caught him almost cold and pressed the button. The guns started to rage and then suddenly clunked off impotently. Splinter swore profoundly.

"What's the matter?" Jackson asked from behind the pilot's seat.

"I told you to stay and watch our tail!" Splinter roared. "We're all done. No more ammunition. Why the devil can't you reload for me?"

He saw the Focke-Wulf swing around just under him as if making up its mind to return to the fray.

"You can still get him," Jackson suggested as he tugged at his mustache thoughtfully. "You have *two* engines, you know."

"Two engines? What's that got to do with it? We haven't any ammo in the guns!"

"All right! Give it to him with one of your engines," old Jackson advised with a crafty leer. "You'll still have another— to get home."

"I don't get . . ." Splinter halted as the impact of the suggestion went home with the smack of a breech block. "But . . . but I might louse it up. And you haven't a parachute."

"You won't louse it up. You mustn't think that way," Jackson reprimanded him. "You're sure of getting back—if you do a clean job. We've got to get another, haven't we?"

Splinter swallowed a rising argument as he saw the Focke-Wulf starting up after him again. There was a chance, and there was merit in what old Jackson had said. You *can* get away on one engine, if you wrap it up properly.

"Hang on *Mister* Jackson!"

He nosed her down, swung over into a sharp turn, and raged after the single-seater. The Nazi pilot saw him coming, and developed a new idea that had the belligerent one beat a mile. You live a long time, if you know when to get out.

"You've got to time it nicely, you know," Jackson cautioned over Splinter's shoulder. "Just nip his rudder and elevators and he's left with his trousers down."

Splinter grinned. "You Pip, Squeak, and Wilfred guys, and your screwy ideas."

The Beaufighter went at it full tilt as Splinter gave her nearly all there was left on the throttle gate. He was on top of the Nazi fighter before he realized it, but a restraining dab on the left rudder pedal held him on course and brought the starboard engine into line.

The night fighter danced momentarily in the Focke-Wulf's

slip stream and Splinter rammed the throttles up to the last notch. For a long, screaming second the two diving planes held a courting dragonfly position, and then Splinter risked all with another slight rudder adjustment and waited for one of his own prop blades to lance through and skewer him to the wall of the cockpit.

There was a metallic thump, a flash of splintered light, and something struck the side of the Beaufighter's flanks with a slam of battered metal. The starboard engine wolfed at the elevator surfaces of the Focke-Wulf and left the snagged ends of gobbled metal gleaming in the exhaust glare.

The Focke-Wulf snapped over on her back.

"Nothing to it," old Jackson said, as glass from the cockpit hatch showered him. "There he goes in a lovely spin!"

The Beaufighter's prop staggered a few uncertain revolutions. The starboard engine spat conclusively over the lip of the engine cowling, and quit. Splinter zoomed her up, reached for a lever, and set a new adjustment on the fin to take up the extra torque of the port engine. Finally she leveled off, collecting her dignity like a blousy old charwoman who has collided unexpectedly with a buttress of the law.

Splinter took her off, clanking and wabbling.

"You see what I mean," old Jackson expounded, "when I say things are cushy in this war? I mean to say, you have *two* engines."

"You mean to say," Splinter corrected, "I *had* two engines. Now if only we have some luck. . ."

They put down a flare path for Splinter and old Jackson half an hour after the others got in. The battered Beaufighter crabbed in with a dithering approach and came to an accordion-pleated landing. A tractor chugged out complainingly and dragged them to a dispersal bay.

"You see what I mean?" old Jackson continued to say. "Two engines!"

Morse, the wing commander, and the adjutant were standing

there, bundled up in their greatcoats, when Jackson and Splinter climbed down. The mechanics tugged at a great chunk of control surface that had become jammed behind the broken-bladed prop.

"That's our confirmation on the fourth," Splinter said before anyone asked him. "Old Jackson had a glorious idea—and it worked!"

"I'd say it was a slab of Nazi rudder," the Winco stated with studied authority. "You must have slogged into one of them."

"Glory! That's what I've been reporting all the way back!" Splinter fumed. "Jackson kidded me into it and I think he ought to get a D.F.C. It was his idea."

"Just what he needs in front of his Pip, Squeak, and Wilfred," Morse added. "At any rate, we'll let him ride with us when we get the Moocher back."

"What happened to Warburton?" young Dingley demanded as he remembered the Consequences report.

"Oh, him. He brought Wells back with a chunk of flak in his shoulder. Then he went over to Control to see about their stockings," Skipper Morse explained with a hopeless pass at nothing.

"Are you starting that, too?" old Jackson asked as he steadied himself on Morse's shoulder.

"No. It's a straight line. He's been working on it for some time with his brother back home. They've arrived at last—a couple of dozen pairs of silk stockings."

Splinter peeped like a leaky valve. "Gone over to Control?"

"Sure. They're presents for the girls. If we don't get some Jerry trade after this—well, Warburton ain't all he's cracked up to be."

"I think I like that Warburton chap," old Jackson chimed in. "What a war!"

What You Do at Twenty-two

DAVID BRYCE fervently hoped he would never be anything but twenty-two. It was an age one should never pass. Twenty-one had been a washout: Steve had gone, and his going had left a cold, hollow fear. The attainment of majority simply meant that David must assume all worldly obligations, legal responsibilities, and declare a loyalty to a political party. Twenty-one produced a frightening period when one stepped across a chasm between the uncertainty of adolescence and the heart-stopping status where you no longer hid behind the irresponsibility of youth.

It was grand to be twenty-two—the golden age where a man is at his physical peak, undaunted by the threats of failure. Not that one shirked responsibilities, for they were all there in their knife-edged facets; but responsibilities at twenty-two were mere goals or pinnacles of attainment. It was like finding oneself a member of the first Air Corps squadron and trusted to fly the new Rapier fighter.

All that and falling in love with Dinky Draper can happen only to guys of twenty-two.

Bryce had heard about the Rapier the day he graduated from primary training at Randolph Field; General Arnold had mentioned it cautiously with that gay twinkle in his blue eyes. But that was when Bryce was twenty-one, and things are beyond reach. The general had also mentioned a new bomber and something about a hush-hush air cannon. They were always saying things like that to lads of twenty-one on graduation, but no one ever expected to *see* a Rapier. The Brass Hats always promised things at pass-out ceremonies.

But today David Bryce was twenty-two and flying a Rapier on defensive patrol. He stared ahead at the one bearing the flight leader's markings—that was Captain Jeff Sprague.

Sprague was a flight commander, but he wasn't twenty-two—he was an old man of twenty-eight with none of the enthusiasm for new equipment. He'd probably experienced all that back in 1938 when he was first allowed to try out one of the latest P-36's. That was a long time ago, and he had probably forgotten what it felt like to be twenty-two. The captain couldn't see the beauty of the Rapier, or sense the ecstasy of flying something that might be faster than anything else in the world. He couldn't appreciate the satisfaction of sitting behind a power plant that was revolutionizing aerial warfare, or glory in the battery of heavy-caliber guns faired so beautifully into the Rapier's wing.

You had to be twenty-two, with enthusiasm—not responsibility—to appreciate all these things.

Jeff Sprague was a broad-shouldered man who fitted the Rapier's cockpit so snugly that he sometimes wondered. He cursed his luck that he should draw a ship like this. The Air Force overseas could provide P-40's, Lightnings, Airacobras, or even Thunderbolts, but he had to be tagged for Rapiers! Sure, the Rapier had everything, and then some—but what could you do about it? You couldn't go across the Ditch and raise hell. You couldn't take chances on offensive sweeps. You couldn't escort bombers like other guys, and run up a record. You were flying a Rapier, and Rapiers were very new and very hush-hush; any guy taking chances that might let the enemy get possession of a Rapier and its secrets was taking plenty of chances with his bars.

There is little enthusiasm at twenty-eight. You're getting old at twenty-eight and a captaincy at twenty-eight isn't even peanuts in a first-class war. There are two ways of getting promotion in wartime, and the other one doesn't matter. You don't get chest hardware, and you certainly cannot get Messerschmitts or Junkers, wet-nursing a new type—and I mean a *new* type.

But not only Rapiers: Sprague was saddled with young Bryce and Ken Harkness. Bryce still shuddered at what had happened to his brother—that would be Steve Bryce, a service test pilot who had pulled the wings off a Maverick P-50 at Farmingdale. That would have been all right, but his chute hadn't opened. Young Bryce quaked openly every time he snapped on his harness. Sprague knew young Bryce would never take chances—not even on defensive patrols.

Harkness was more mature; twenty-four or so and a good pilot, but Harkness was one of those engineering M.I.T. guys who figured things on a slide rule and tried to run his world by tables and mathematics. Harkness was not a *fighter* pilot; he could always prove that certain stresses were too risky in certain combat maneuvers. A new Rapier was just another mathematical experiment to Harkness—like a new micrometer or an armament formula sent over by the RAF research mob.

The first time Harkness flew a Rapier he went up with fifty rounds and did a test dive on a drogue target. When he came down and discovered that he had put forty-two rounds into the sleeve he was mad, and spent nearly a week trying to figure out why the other eight had missed. Sprague wondered if Ken would worry that much if he missed a Focke-Wulf 190 the first time he let drive at one.

Harkness was also sensitive. He worried about young Bryce and tried to erase the parachute business from his mind, but the gesture was overdone and Dave resented it; in fact, he resented everything about Harkness. There was that unconsciously superior air he assumed when they talked about the hush-hush features of the Rapier. Ken explained to him why the supercharger was on the secret list, and tried to scribble out the formula of the new alloy that went into the impeller vane. And there was another lecture on the clever staggering of the guns and the ammunition feeds, which allowed two extra guns in a wing that had no greater span than a Spitfire.

Sprague tried to break it up one day with: "Never mind all that. You can't get out and fix it at operating height. All we have to remember is not to be sucked in too far, so that we put one down on an occupied field for these Nazi guys to go over. They're the orders, and we're elected!"

Major Merrill reminded them again that some RAF dope had put down a brand-new Mosquito bomber on a Swiss field a few days before, and there was hell to pay.

"We won't get Heinies out of this," Sprague grumbled. "All we'll get is flying hours, and you can get those ferrying bombers —and with better pay!"

The three gleaming Rapiers huddled in closer as Captain Sprague swung them clear of the resticted area around Woolwich, and then he waggled his wings, so both Harkness and Bryce listened in on their sets.

Sprague was getting a warning from their Operations shed.

"To Number 1 Section. Claridge to Number 1 Section... Formation enemy Dornier 17-Z's attacking Gravesend loading docks. Twelve-plus at least. Take it, Section 1."

"Get that, you guys?" Sprague demanded.

Harkness came up with: "Dornier 17-Z's, Cappy? They're the new four-place jobs, superseding the Do-115's. They have six guns and can sure hand it out!"

"Good! So can we! You stick tight with me, Bryce."

"She has a belly turret, and guns firing from ports on each side," Harkness rattled on.

Bryce was glad he was twenty-two. All he had to worry about was to hold his position and bang away at every target that slipped across his sights. That's all there was to it. Sprague had to worry about how far they went, and Harkness was stewing about belly guns and turrets set in the sides of a new German bomber. Who cared? They were flying Rapiers, and nothing could keep up with a Rapier—and they didn't have to go too far over. This could be a real birthday party.

Sprague brought them around smartly. The three fighters hoisted their port wings against the late-afternoon sunlight, patted the glare off, and went screaming away for Gravesend. The river below wriggled and seemed to throw a matted carpet of flotsam up on its banks, and the tangle became something one studied on an aerial photo. A few lazy blobs hung disconsolately from their curved cables, and in the patchwork pattern below were dozens of kite-balloon winches mounted on lorries with heavy wire canopies over them—just in case Jerry bashed into a cable and let the tangle down on the WAAF girls who manned the defenses.

"Winches wun by wenches," Dave Bryce said over and over, and wondered why the silly lisped line came to his mind and tongue whenever he saw a barrage balloon.

"What are you talking about?" Sprague snapped. "Keep buttoned up, Bryce, and stay in position, even though we tangle with these guys. You stay in position!"

Bryce frowned and wished he could remember to snap off his throat mike. Sprague always caught him when he was enjoying something ridiculous; but Sprague was twenty-eight, Dave reminded himself. You get old and crotchety at that age. You have two bars on your collar tabs, and you have a lot of dopey responsibility. At twenty-two you are tickled with a second-looie bar, and you can kid yourself you're fighting the war your way, even though you have to stay in position and cover the captain's tail.

The set crackled again and Ken Harkness said: "How about down there to the right, Skipper?"

Bryce could see from his position that Ken had his hatch cover back and had one eye cocked over the starboard side. He was putting the old calipers on something below. "I mean,

Skipper—cutting across for Tilbury. That's Tilbury on the other side, isn't it?"

"I wouldn't know what it is," Sprague spat back. "All I know is that there're ten or a dozen Dorniers down there. Let's go to work!"

Bryce tried to figure out what it was Harkness was talking about. He steadied himself on his seat pack and took the peel-off signal from Sprague. He glanced over at Harkness again, and Ken signaled him down after the skipper. That meant Sprague would get first shot at the Dorniers and Dave would be expected to tail him on through. Harkness could either hold the line or take a couple of deflection shots at the outer-position bombers.

Dave still couldn't see them, even after he had kicked his ship over and peeled off after Sprague. As the Rapier straightened out, he hung tight against his belt and for the first time realized what was expected of him. They were actually on their way down to shoot someone. There were Dorniers down there— Jerry bombers with six guns, according to Harkness. They had been after the new docks at Gravesend. This could have been over Kiska, Guadalcanal, or even Bizerte; it just happened that they were flying Rapiers over a place called Gravesend. It was all part of the same war. . . . Gravesend, somewhere along the Thames.

"Where the hell are you going, Bryce?" someone bawled over the set. "Sprague is heading down there!"

Bryce knew that that must be Harkness. He was supposed to be somewhere behind. The pressure of the dive and the scream of slip steam seemed to be draining everything out of him. He tried to answer, but no sound came, and he struggled into the other corner of his seat to see what Sprague was doing.

The skipper was not to be seen!

"What happened, kid? Blackout on the peel-off?" Harkness asked. Bryce twisted around again and was relieved to find that the subleader had moved down and was hurtling earthward beside him. Harkness made an exaggerated gesture with his thumb, curving it over to the right while he kicked over in a tight quarter turn and led the way. Dave corkscrewed after him, and together they slammed straight into the mess below.

The Dorniers were heading for the Estuary now, and Sprague was racing wildly after them. The signal strength was faltering on Dave's set, but he could hear the skipper shouting for them to tie up with him. Streaks of converging tracer from the dorsal turrets of the enemy bombers were snapping at Sprague's tail surfaces. That made Bryce wince, as for the first time he saw the full optical effect of hostile gunfire. If one of those spitters snapped into Sprague's wing root, there was a swell chance his tanks would go up. They could go up, even though they did have what the manufacturers called fireproof tanks. You hit 'em right, and you put in a long, jagged gash that no self-sealing compound will blubber over. If Sprague got a flamer, he'd have to take to the silk.

The thought planted a heavy cold pebble between the layers of tissue that held in Bryce's belly. He didn't want to think about Steve, but with Sprague ripping in blindly like that, anything could happen.

Dave wound his way into position again, flying with jerky, automatic movements. His mind was not on his gun button or his formation position. He caught himself asking Steve what it felt like—what he said when he discovered the rip cord wouldn't release his parachute over Farmingdale. "Couldn't you have twisted around somehow and pulled the stuff out with your hands, Steve?" he asked for the umpteenth time. "You can pull it out, can't you, Steve, if you can get the flaps open?"

"Stop that chatter!" Captain Sprague growled back at him over the short ether lane that separated them. "Stop that senseless chatter and stick to my tail, Bryce. Where the devil were you, anyway?"

"It's all right, Cappy!" Ken Harkness assured from the other flipper position.

Why did Harkness have to assume that Big Brother attitude? If Harkness knew so much, why couldn't he tell him what had happened to Steve's chute? All he ever said was that it had been improperly packed and insinuated that test pilots often get careless about little things because they have so many other matters to worry about. That was twenty-four being patronizing to twenty-two.

"Twenty-four is a boorish age," Dave decided. "You're neither one thing nor the other." Sprague was twenty-eight and crowding his load figures with worry and responsibility. At twenty-four, you're taking yourself too seriously. Twenty-two is the age to be.

Sprague was charging into a Vee of three Dorniers and his guns snapped serpent tongues of slitted flame and broke through the converging fire of the rear turret gunners. There was a tallow-colored bulge of smoke and a forked blade of flame as a Dornier's port engine ripped out and hurled itself across the sky. A chunk of wing cranked up, flapped over, and smacked the side of the bomber's fuselage with the crash of a depth charge.

"That's one for you, Skipper!" Ken Harkness cheered.

The three Rapiers raged over the broken formation, and Sprague took them skyward with a triumphant zoom. Dave wondered whether he should have tried a shot at one of the bombers in an upper layer. He mumbled something indistinct, fumbled with his reflector-sight knob, and set the ring for a wide wing span—just in case he got a chance.

Sprague took them around again, and Bryce saw three flopping figures tumble away from the burning bomber. He gripped the top of his stick hard, and heard his own guns rattling. He stared ahead with the realization that he had frozen onto his button. His earphones screamed at him, but he could not make out the words. He still watched to see whether the three parachutes would open.

"Cut those guns!" Sprague finally broke in.

The involuntary burst had ruled several sparky parallel lines across the shaggy quilt of Surrey below. It wasn't much of a burst, but enough to enrage Sprague and jerk Bryce out of his blue funk. Besides, all three parachutes had opened. Well, two had, at any rate. Dave could not see the third; he had to take that one for granted.

"We'll keep after them," Sprague announced. "And don't waste your stuff that way, Bryce. You stay with me!"

The formation of bombers had sped on and was crossing the muddy Estuary. The Thanet ack-ack guns opened on them, and they splayed out wide and made the most of their stripped weight. Their bombs had been jettisoned somewhere and they had the speed of lean-flanked greyhounds. To stay with them and carry out their routine attack maneuvers would take all the Rapiers had. The Dornier pilots had only to hold their depressed course and head for somewhere north of Calais. The Rapiers had to climb for position, evade the turret gunfire, and ram in for sharp dive attacks, and clear again. All this took time, and seconds were precious when the occupied coast was only minutes away.

Bryce could see the scraggy beaches of Dunkirk and the shadowy warp and weft of barbed wire, the rusting hulks that had once formed part of a deliverance fleet—an epic he had read about so abstractedly nearly three years before. He was nineteen then and a war three thousand miles away couldn't compete with the prospects of getting a tennis letter or the decision to be made as to whether he should go to Dartmouth or Princeton.

Bryce moved in again and glanced across at Harkness. Sprague was jinking them all over the sky, darting in and out in an effort to drive home another attack. Ken was putting on the twenty-four business and looking worried. They were well out over the Ditch now, and Sprague undoubtedly was bullheading his way into trouble. Harkness shook his head when he caught Dave's eye.

"Let's have another smack at them," Sprague called. "We'll each pick one this time, and then beat it."

"You're too far—I mean we're beyond our area now, aren't we, Skipper?" Harkness said as they moved around again.

"We'll take the three-ship element off to the left. We'll take one apiece," Sprague continued. "Let's go!"

Dave Bryce stared at his gun button and made certain the safety collar was off. He fingered nervously under the cheek flaps of his helmet and then slipped off his right glove. The old fear arose again as he stared under his left elbow at the heavy D-shaped rip-cord ring snuggled in its webbing pocket. He hoped he'd never have to pin his hopes on that thing.

Sprague was climbing now, while the Nazi gunners snapped off short bursts calculated to keep them at their distance. David and Ken watched their leader thumb the sun before he curled into a position which enabled them to enjoy some cover from the watery yellow ball.

"This is a mug's game," Dave gulped. "We couldn't get back now—if anything happened." He tried to talk himself into a fighting mood but his words were dazed and jaded phrases. He tried to work up a gleam of hate for the enemy insignia that glazed from the wings and bodies of the bombers, but the three men who had been forced to take to the silk left him with a hidden wound.

The reflector sight gleamed a weak neon marker in the glass of his windshield and became a circular stamp of cowardice. He tried to remember what letter Hawthorne had used in his novel to mark the breast of a woman. He wondered if all fighter pilots would come out of the war with a scarlet circle burned indelibly into their foreheads. He spat the fear of that into an indistinct corner, and banked sharply with Sprague.

"You can't miss, you guys!" taunted Sprague. "Take 'em— one, two, *three!*"

"We're a hell of a long way over, Skipper," Harkness bleated.

But Sprague was charged with volts of promised glory. He zoomed, banked sharply, and poised high for the attack. Harkness and Bryce came around after him, slithered through a tilted bank, and splayed out into their positions. Together, they roared down at the outer spearhead of bombers.

What happened a second later lifted the heavy pebble from the pit of Bryce's stomach and punched it up into his throat. He opened his mouth wide and gasped, as, ahead, he saw Sprague's Rapier blow apart. The wings shot out, leaving hacked wounds of fractured metal. A toothed circlet of flame whipped around ahead of the windshield as the motor cowling ripped away. Smoke mushroomed back over the tail assembly.

Dave didn't yell—he simply hoiked his kite gently over the stalled wreckage and said, "They got the Skipper—a flamer!" He practically whispered it as though it were on the secret list— like the Rapier. He nosed down gently, put his scarlet sight smack on the Dornier's dorsal turret, and pressed the button.

He felt cool now. It was like having been bathed off with soft cotton and alcohol. Somehow he fitted the seat better, and the parachute pack was comfortable. The distance to the rudder pedals had been adjusted and all he had to do was treadle lightly, left or right, and the Rapier responded with the certainty of a show mount in a Good Hands contest.

Bryce was moving in and out, serene and composed, as though he had been doing all this for months. From one three-ship element to another he darted, snapping off short bursts—amazed at the ease with which this battle maneuver was accomplished. There were bombers in trouble everywhere. One was in flames, skating across the sky and shaking its great head like a quirted mustang. The whole scene was tied together with long, sparkling lengths of gilt-package cord. That these might be incendiary shells from Nazi 20-mm. guns did not occur to Dave. He just whispered: "They got the Skipper—a flamer!"

Then Ken Harkness's voice cried in anguish over the set: "Sprague's down! He hit damned hard, too. Smack into the sea. They won't get his crate!"

Bryce shagged back into the melee again. He pressed off another burst at a Dornier. Pieces of metal flipped up and fluttered away in glinting sheets.

"I suppose I should write Dinky and tell her all about this," Dave said as he cleared a great chunk of wing panel fluttering across the sky.

Dinky was Hope Draper, a one-hundred-and-ten-pounder who carried plenty of authority with Dave. Not exactly a Powers model, but she had stopped A.T. Flight 84 at Valdosta where Dave had finished off before going overseas. Dinky was in some civic organization that helped the young married group find apartments, and drove her own station wagon for the U.S.O. crowd there. Dinky's old gent was someone important in a government setup that was trying to straighten out the synthetic-rubber tangle.

Dinky had caught up with Bryce shortly after Steve's affair. Steve's crack-up had almost washed David out, but Dinky hauled him off one night on some excuse, and by the time they had pawed over a chicken blue plate at Bebe's Barn, their future was pretty well accounted for.

"You're not going to let this spoil your life," Dinky ordered. Instinctively, Bryce looked for at least an oak leaf of authority on her jacket. "After all, I have something in this kitty. Suppose Steve had gotten it over Buna or Berlin; you wouldn't have quit then. He could have been leading an active-service squadron, you know. You *could* assume he just checked out and left you to carry on."

"Some of us might be checked out as instructors," he suggested feebly.

That was where Dinky poured on the sauce; where she drew down her chunk of glory. She should have been awarded a Congressional Medal of Honor.

"That's out!" she stated. "We're not in the 'married-with-dependents' class yet. That can wait until after the war. Someone has to instruct—but not you. You're a natural-formation pilot, David. I get around, and I know what I hear."

"I guess you're right, Dinky," he agreed, suddenly remembering Steve.

"Listen, David. Instructors grow old too soon—too much responsibility. If they are good, someone turns them into test pilots. You're straight fighter material—for the duration. Not instructors, David. They stay in, and don't even grow old gracefully."

He nodded dumbly and listened to the juke box swing on another record. As he turned and watched the tone arm drop, he capitulated with: "Okay, Dinko! Let's dance. When I get overseas, I'll drop you a line and tell you how good *you* are."

She reached up and kissed him. "You just write, sweetheart."

Harkness went past him, punching off short bursts at everything with black crosses on it. The Dornier formation was scattered all over the sky and a few headed into muffin pats of cloud for safety.

Bryce snapped in his set and called the subleader, "You sure Jeff cleared and made the water, Ken? You're not going over any farther, are you?"

But Harkness was vitalized with his new authority which flailed him into chasing the bombers deep into the Pas de Calais area. There was nothing to do but tail him, according to instructions—anything could happen now.

"Come on, Bryce!" Harkness yelled. "We've got these guys cold. We can pick them off by numbers."

That was the general line Sprague had used. Guys of twenty-four, Bryce decided, are in the same category as pilots with about three hundred hours in their logbooks. They're in a bad spot. They've lost all their initial caution and haven't picked up the full weight of experience. They're trying to justify themselves and prove they're ready for command and responsibility. Harkness was in a spot where he needed someone to level him off.

Bryce palmed the throttle knob up and flailed after his subleader. Ken was trying to break up another three-ship formation, and Bryce found himself riding wing tip to wing tip between the lead Dornier's two wing men—a swell spot for trouble.

Two dorsal turret gunners snapped their guns around and let him have it. The Rapier rang with the impact of the hate. Ken's Dornier target up front snapped over hard and coughed a black orchid of smoke. She rolled over on her back and stuck a wing tip full into the port engine of an accompanying Dornier.

Bryce never knew how he cleared the mess, but he came out smoking; the cockpit went into a black-out, and he gulped a lungful. Then he remembered to pull his oxygen mask up and rip back the hatch cover.

"This is it!" he muttered.

Harkness's voice came over the earphones shouting something about making sure his safety pin was clear. That meant he was to make certain he could get rid of the harness the minute he hit the ground.

"Hit the silk, kid!" Harkness was saying. "I'll cover you on the way down—and best of luck!"

Bryce smoothed what he had left into an easy spiral and looked over the side. His starboard wing tank was spuming a jagged pennon of flame and eating away at the dural skin of the wing covering. He tugged at the safety catch of his belt and looked over the side. That was France—or Belgium—down there. She might not burn clean out—it might be a good idea to stay with her long enough to make sure.

"You can't stay there, Bryce!" Harkness screamed again. "You're all right, aren't you? Get clear, kid!"

"They're not going to get me this way," Bryce muttered with a quick glance across his instrument board. He saw the two tank gauges, and shoved his gloved fist through a licking of flame and switched over to the port tank. His young mind calculated fast, his eyes separated minutes from the clock and assayed them against the vernier markings on the fuel gauge. Forty-seven minutes against the starboard wing tankage didn't leave too much, but maybe he could sit this out.

"You dope!" Harkness raged again. "Why don't you check out? You'll be back over the Ditch in a minute!"

"Sure. That's right. Maybe I can make the Ditch the way Jeff did. They won't be able to get the Rapier there. Maybe with the wheels partly down I can belly-flop her in and not get it too bad. They'll come out and snatch me, but they won't get the kite!"

That was one reasoning Bryce was working up, but over the other wire he was trembling with the fear of having to take to the silk. Steve took to the silk once—and it didn't balloon for him.

Harkness wouldn't be able to understand that. He was twenty-four. You have to be twenty-two to figure fast with time against tankage. Harkness could figure—but not up here without a slide rule. Two years can make a difference.

Bryce glanced over again, drew a leg back from the flame, and realized he was staring at two naked compression ribs. He could see the breeches of three guns, too. The flame was gobbling the wing surface as if it were tinfoil. Two former ribs had been torched into something resembling a small hank of washline. If the main spar was getting any of that heat ...

Something was tightening about his right leg and he kicked at the hole through which the flame was spearing into the cockpit. He wondered if he could block it off with the sole of his boot.

"Fifty minutes is top time under normal operating conditions," he argued with what dials he could see on the instrument panel. "Why couldn't Harkness think of that?"

But Harkness's reasoning had been impaired by the sight of Bryce's flamer. To gamble tankage against time never entered his mind. "Why don't you clear, kid? Why don't you ..."

There was a choked convulsion up front, as the Rapier's engine took over the supply from the port tank. Bryce listened and huddled over as far as he could get—the flame was boring gimlet holes through the sole of his right foot now. He leaned out farther and saw the Ditch below and wondered how long he had been clear of the enemy coast.

"Nearly fifty minutes and she's still burning raw stuff," he grumbled. "Shows how guys like Harkness can get their figures mixed. Fifty minutes, they say, but maybe they allow a few more as a margin of safety." He quaked at that. The margin of safety might make him take to the silk yet.

He looked about and saw Harkness riding tight on his wing tip. The subleader was doing mysterious things with his hands—pointing at something and then holding his palms out, but Bryce's set was out and he could not hear him.

"I know! I know! I'll wash her out as soon as I'm certain we're in the clear. You don't have to tell me."

He peered about for the button that would lower his landing gear. He was puzzled to find the cockpit clear of smoke. He tried to drag his right foot over to the rudder pedal but the rubber sole was stuck fast to a blackened metal former. He tugged again and tore it clear—no flame snapped through.

"Wait a minute," he deliberated, and looked at the clock again. "Fifty-one minutes..."

He moved over and glanced down at the starboard wing root and suddenly Harkness's voice came through again. "Maybe if you take it easy, she'll hold out. That main spar has a safety factor of about ten. Maybe we can get you in, kid."

"Here he comes again," Bryce growled. "A few minutes ago he was telling me to dive out the window!"

"Now, don't lose your head, kid," the subleader bleated. "We'll get you back if you take it easy."

"Don't you worry about me, Harkness. I'm sticking with this hulk all the way home. I'm not dropping her in the Ditch, and

I'm not taking to the silk. She's mine, and I'm taking her in—all the way."

Harkness put on his act all the way back, and went in first to give his version of the patrol. He had the meat wagon out near the runway, and he posed with a studied air of authority. As Bryce flew over once to see if any special signal had been laid out, a large chunk of daylight could be seen through his starboard wing.

"That's nothing," Harkness explained. "She's got a main spar with a safety factor of about ten. I told him he'd be okay. I was afraid he'd lose his head and jump. You have to think for some of these kids, you know."

The Rapier came in fast, for want of flap area, and Bryce just saved her from ground-looping by judicious use of his brakes. He brought her around and wabbled up to the dispersal area, and before they could get to him, he shoved one blackened leg out stiffly. A ground crew corporal took one look, and walked away.

Harkness rushed up and grabbed him as he tottered on the wing. "Nice going, kid. I'm glad you didn't chuck it and take to the silk. You know, they give guys D.F.C.'s for efforts like this."

Being only twenty-two, young Bryce couldn't think of anything heroic in response. The war correspondents have to think up those lines. He just said, "What's that? The Distinguished *Frying* Cross?"

Seven Must Return

Greasy Neale, a Stirling bomber, had left Number 208's station at Sywell shortly after dark. Her objective was the Siemens works in Berlin. This joy ride produces about six hours of mental anguish, or abstract deliberation, for the seven men cooped up inside the metal walls of that hideous but very effective piece of equipment.

For half of the journey seven men huddle above eight tons of bombs—that works out to one ton apiece and an extra ton for a chap they call George King who lives in Buckingham Palace.

The sentimentalists are prone to magnify the community spirit or *esprit de corps* aboard military aircraft, and those with space in periodicals open to them often confuse the individual fighting spirit of men with cooperative devotion to duty.

Aboard *Greasy Neale* there are eighty-four feet of swaying catwalk between Sergeant Tim Bollinger in the nose turret and the four-gun Browning station in the tail, and just what community of spirit Bollinger can have with Air Gunner Montague-Bates is not very clear. As a matter of fact, Tim is quite certain that one of these nights Monty will cork off and let a Heinkel punch its initials in them before Mike Jobbins in the dorsal turret can take defensive action.

Jobbins is no bargain. There's a bit of Sir Francis Drake in Jobbins—he's wonky about lawn bowls and spends most of his time, when he should be At Alert, working out new theories of being "on the jack" from backhand play.

Flight Lieutenant Edgar Hammersley is rated as captain of aircraft and there are times when he lets the rest of them know it. The Number Two pilot, Jimmie Kegworth, hopes that one of these nights something unpleasant will happen to Hammersley that will give Jimmie a chance to bring *Greasy Neale* home. He figures there'd be a D.F.C. in that effort, at least.

"My job," Flying Officer Dyce once explained to a WAAF section leader, "is comparable to that of a destroyer flotilla leader. I have my fight-control bridge, I assume full control of the engineering problems, and during an engagement I'm chief gunnery officer. Takes a bit of doing, you know."

The air gunners hope he walks into a prop some dark night.

Dickie Steadman considers himself indispensable, too. Steadman is the navigator bomb aimer, but don't let him start telling you how he guided a Wellington across the Alps and bombed Turin. He'll bend your ear double about a new gadget he's working on. A line shooter, really.

With this litigious lot aboard *Greasy Neale*, it is difficult to understand how they complete a mission of any sort. Still, they have logged some tidy shows and somehow they usually get back.

There must be a reason for it.

Steadman took his first fix out of Sywell when they were over Bury Saint Edmunds. He got a vector of 174 and crossed the coast at Lowestoft. Hunched in tight to his table, he jotted down the figures and pawed nervously with a pair of parallel rulers. Through a small port he could see two engines and the disc of splintered light swirled in by the prop blades. If the cuff on one of those blades went out, he stood a fair chance of being skewered to the wall behind him like a specimen on a naturalist's pin. Dickie never stopped fearing that fate, and wondered if Dyce had any critical figures on the possibility of a propeller throwing a blade.

He got up, took up his new sextant, pottered past Dyce who was at his panel, and assured himself, after taking a sight on Pollux, that Venus was in her appointed position six degrees south.

He hurried forward again, grabbed his mike, and reported

position to Hammersley in the control compartment above. The pilot answered, and Dickie watched the leading edge of the wing warp out slightly, and again his eye caught the sheen of the inboard engine prop. He squinted at it, gagged on an acidy tang of fear, and tried to forget it in the tabulation of a second set of figures. All this reminded him that when he got back he must obtain that appointment with the Air Commodore so that he could present his theory of rapid position finding as computed with his new sextant.

He mumbled and recited his examples again, poked his pencil at the fine figures, and hoped he'd get a chance tonight to work against the present Air Ministry syllabus. If Hammersley took her through on a reasonable course he might get a chance to use both systems and have them to present to the Air Commodore.

The figures were clicking already, but so was that damned prop out there. He glanced at the flailing arms of the great three-bladed airscrew and computed his chances of being hit. He took the number of revolutions per minute, estimated the segment his body occupied outside the arc, which gave him the figures on the chances against one blade. He multiplied it by three and the result was terrifying.

"Whew! Engine speed 2,900 rpm," he wheezed. "I've got to get a check tonight, and get back. They might appoint me as an instructor and I won't have to sit opposite this blasted bayonet machine any longer." Dickie Steadman worked up a good case for their returning safely that night. . . .

Hammersley also considered a set of figures as he sat behind the big wheel and watched the altimeter needle climb to the big figure six. His computations were in his logbook. They had been multiplying by the week. Another six hours would put him in a favorable spot for his squadron leader's rank. That brought up prospects of a command. Two hundred operational hours ought to put him over with the Group captain who had been dropping hints concerning a new squadron in the Group.

"Just you wait, Rayl," he had assured the girl in the snack

bar at the Fountain Hotel in Bletchley two nights before. "One more Berlin show and they'll have to give me my S/L."

The girl considered this as she speared a tiny sausage. Her name was Raylton Blandford and she wore the uniform of the Auxiliary Territorial Service. Her hair was the color of eighty-year-old sherry and reflected the burnished glow of the candle sconces. A ribbon of the Military Medal on her tunic was a reminder of the night she had taken a lorry through Coventry.

"All that matters," she said in a voice tuned to a far-off vestry ball, "is that you get back. I can wait for—the other. We can both wait."

"But we've waited so long, Rayl," Hammersley pleaded again. "If I can get that extra bit of braid, I'm sure we could manage it, and feel on the safe side."

"Is there a safe side? You'll still have to go night after night. This waiting is nothing compared to the hours we wait for you, trip after trip. That's all that seems to be left, the minutes of pain and pleasure listening for you to rumble in. We sit in the transport yard and try to count the exhaust streaks, but there are so many, and so few come back—sometimes."

"I suppose it is ghastly," he consoled her. "Kegworth and I talk about it sometimes. Queer bloke, Kegworth."

"Queer? There must be something to a lad who gets the affection from a dog that he does. I sit in the dark out there and wait for you, and Meg huddles near me and waits for Jimmie. Somehow, she knows before I do."

"Let's talk about us," Hammersley parried. "Let's chance it all and slip up to town and get a special license the minute my promotion comes through."

"You've got enough to worry about, being responsible for the others, without worrying about a bride." She smiled doubtfully. "Soldiers shouldn't marry during wartime, Edgar."

He hunched forward, covered her small sturdy hand with his, and closed his warm fingers. "You're right, Rayl, but let's chance it. Let's go up to town for the weekend and get married. The rank will come through."

"I suppose you should have an objective at both ends of your run," she agreed, as she hid her eyes with her free hand. "I'll chance it. I'll see my section leader in the morning."

His eyes gleamed in anticipation and he whispered, "You're a brick, Rayl. Don't worry, I'll get back."

Her capitulation was reflected in detail on the windscreen of the big Stirling as Flight Lieutenant Hammersley guided the machine into the flak that came up from the ack-ack barrages outside Ijmuiden. No curtain of Krupp steel would prevent his getting back tonight.

"I'll have a look see about before the band strikes up," Jimmie Kegworth said, and slipped out of his seat.

Hammersley turned and stared at his copilot as though he wondered how he came to be part of his snug party at the Fountain Hotel.

Jimmie had to hang on going through the bulkhead for Hammersley was throwing the bus all over the shop now. The flak was stamping great batik designs against the sable canopy.

"Jelly-belly, eh?" Kegworth called to Steadman.

"Don't know whether we're over Haarlem or Hong Kong. Might just as well sling a dart at the chart when he jinks her about like this." Steadman threw out his arms in a semicircle and scooped his instruments together.

A double issue of searchlight forked up from Amsterdam, semaphored back and forth twice, steadied, and held the emerald Zuider Zee between the bars of a Victory V.

Jimmie studied Dyce's face as the engineer bloke jotted manifold pressure data in an engine log.

"How're we churning?"

"Any luck at all, and we'll get back all right."

Kegworth's face seemed to lengthen. "Good egg! I've *got* to get back. Meg's about to whelp."

The word "whelp" made Dyce wince—just as if one motor had cut out.

Sergeant Bollinger, who sat at ease before his radio panel, edged over and grabbed Kegworth's arm as he moved farther aft to climb through the main spar frame.

" 'Ad Meg 'ad 'er pups when you left, sir?"

"No. Probably in the morning," Jimmie explained. He glanced at the panel and wondered if he dared contact Sywell and make sure his setter, Meg O'Dawn, was being properly tended by his batman, Crockett. "She'll be all right—I hope."

He moved on through the spar frame and steadied himself against the rest bunk. He squatted on the edge and patted the pillow gently as if he were soothing Meg. He wondered if Crockett would manage a bit of carpet which would give the pups a place to claw at so they could suckle satisfactorily.

"Hang on, Meg," he muttered in the half-light of the wing compartment. "I'll be back, old girl. You just wait for me."

He closed his eyes and saw her again, a beautiful animal, warm and friendly, bearing her condition with regal dignity. She was all he had now, and he was glad he'd broken the station rule and brought her with him. There was nothing left back at Arle. Jerry had taken care of that when he bashed Norwich about. That was after Number 208 had bombed Rostock for the second time. Queer that Jerry should have scored such an unexpected revenge. The cottage had crumbled under the blow and there were two new mounds in a churchyard just down the road.

"Plenty of clean straw, Crockett, old son," he went on with half-closed eyes. "A sponge down within an hour and a gentle toweling. Never mind my kit. That can wait."

A spanking crash outside sent Jimmie leaping off the bunk. *Greasy Neale* was skating all over the sky and Kegworth tripped and went headlong down the companionway, rolled over on his back, and lay staring breathless at the escape hatch in the roof.

Frantic voices came over the intercom demanding that some-one get that swine.

Jimmie crawled along on his hands and knees until he reached the ladder that went up into Jobbins' gun turret. He bellowed something and shoved his hand under the seat and grabbed the gunner's ankle.

"What is it, Jobbins? What's going on out there?"

The turret swung on greased guides and the gunner leaned over and bellowed through his knees: "I'm all right, sir! I shoved him off all right. Think we made him stink a bit . . . Yes, he's wrapping it up."

"Good! Ruddy good, Jobbins!"

Through the oblong ports along the fuselage a scarlet glare threw half-a-dozen magic-lantern sunsets on the opposite wall. They remained stationary at the level of the maintenance plank and then moved slowly upward, thinning out to mere slits of crimson, and then disappeared.

A flamer had gone down, and Jimmie Kegworth staggered back along the catwalk wondering whether Crockett would manage all right.

Greasy Neale steadied again and Hammersley listened intently to advice from Steadman: "We're still on course, Skipper. Osnabrück ahead. Getting considerable drift now. You might bend the vector ten degrees right. One-eight-four."

"Righto! One-eight-four. Gunners report!" Hammersley called, and wondered whether Rayl would like a quiet little spot down Kingston-on-Thames way, or whether she'd risk it properly and stay at the Regal Palace in town.

Sergeant Bollinger listened while Jobbins and Montague-Bates reported their concerted attack on the Messerschmitt 110, and quietly cursed his luck that he had to be on the radio panel while all that was going on. It had been in the cards that Sergeant Bollinger would become a wireless air gunner, since all his life he had enjoyed the questionable role of a Jack-of-all-trades. His long, expressive hands, which were needled with coarse black hair, were deft and accomplished. There had been a time when

he had fancied himself something of a gentleman cracksman. A
Jimmy Valentine, so to speak. He had practiced many hours,
with his fingertips sandpapered almost raw, on the old biscuit tin
Messrs. Umpleby and Ormiston used for a safe. Unfortunately,
he was caught redhanded at this delicate task and promptly
sacked by the chief clerk who completely misunderstood his
innocent intentions.

After that unfortunate escapade Bollinger forswore such sus-
picious experiments and went in for magic and sleight of hand,
the rudiments of which he had gleaned from a sixpenny brochure
purchased one Saturday afternoon when his current hobbies
began to pall.

To cut a longish story short, Sergeant Bollinger was to appear
the following night on the program of the weekly concert party
staged in the N.A.A.F.I. hut, under the glittering billing, "The
Brilliant Bollinger." For weeks he had been practicing the
opening-egg trick, the amazing billiard-ball mystery act, his
especial and dexterous manipulation of a pack of cards, and his
finale (pronounced fee-nar-ley) larrup of legerdemain in which
he poured a goblet of foaming beer from an old petrol tin into
which had been previously sloshed some engine oil, a bottle of
ink, and a jam jar full of disinfectant.

He had scrawled his patter, and mouthed it night after night
when things were a bit slow on the panel. He had made all
arrangements to borrow a dress suit through the station padre
who knew the vicar in the village. His table and the spangled
length of drapery were all ready, and he had diligently polished
up a bit of swagger stick for his wand.

"A chap 'as to look into the future," he told himself many
times. "When this mess is over, we'll all be chucked out with
a bit of blood money, a thirty-shillin' serge suit, and left to
wonder wot there is left to do in civvy life. There won't be any
jobs, because all the gals will 'ave them. I'm lookin' arfter meself,
I am."

There was no question about it. The Brilliant Bollinger *had* to get back tonight.

"You must watch me closely, ladies and gentlemen," he rehearsed again as the searchlights below attempted to pierce the dural and play a giant spot on this Demon of Delusion. "The quickness of the 'and deceives the heye!"

Once the hate simmered down, Dyce computed his tankage, booked the figures with a professional flourish, and then turned gingerly toward his swinging seat and sat down.

There wouldn't be much for him to do now they were in the clear. That is, nothing much to do but worry. He could already see the rubious glow on the horizon, testifying that the Wellingtons had arrived on schedule and scattered their target-marking incendiaries.

Dyce was a tall, shapeless man who might have been assembled from a lot of spare parts; his face was long and smudged with beard, his pants-button eyes were sewn in close together and separated by the receding bridge of a long, ecclesiastical nose.

Aboard *Greasy Neale*, Dyce was a drab workman. On the station and about the mess, he was a swashbuckling figure of raffish splendor and swaggering efficiency. Dyce talked a good war, but once engaged in his appointed tasks over enemy areas, he lost much of his bounce, and the aura of his studied braggadocio was usually filtered into a splutter by the constant apprehension that beset him. Dyce presented a splendid example of that brand of courage which steels a man from displaying his inherent timidity, for fear his fellow men will mark him as a coward.

He sat foundering in a rip tide of realization that only a few feet away in the wings hung three massive bombs, any one of which might suffer premature detonation by a chunk of flak and blow them all to smithereens. The fact that many more of greater power hung in the bomb gallery beneath his feet somehow never entered his mind.

To Dyce, a safe return meant two things. First, it meant that they had got rid of those damned bombs. Dyce hated bombs.

He even distrusted the ammunition in the gun turrets. Explosives were something over which he had no command, no dials, no switches, no pet cocks by which he could influence their actions.

They simply had to get back—all the way back, with empty bomb cells, too. It was a ridiculous rule that bombs were not to be released unless the target was clearly identified. What if there was a bit of indiscriminate bombing? Who cared? The Huns slung the stuff all over the garden when the Spitters got after them. Why take the double chance by bringing back the plum puddings? You could still mess it up if old Hammersley made a squeamish landing.

"I'd put this blasted instrument panel well up front," he had mooned a dozen times. "Ridiculous, placing it here, not five feet from the wing-cell bombs. A man doesn't have a chance here."

There was another angle, too. "And if I had my say, I'd have another set of bomb releases on my panel. How do we know whether Steadman is alive and able to get rid of them when we're dead over? After he yells, 'Bomb doors open!' a devil of a lot can happen."

There was little sense to his fears and imaginings, but he nurtured them for six long, terror-drenched hours. He was never certain of his fate until they were all the way back—with empty bomb cells.

On the other hand, he had his role to play. He was the star turn aboard *Greasy Neale* and he was egoist enough to sense what was expected of him. He had assumed the mantle of Captain Bobadil and he gloried in it. When he returned, they'd all be there, from the Air Commodore down, practically queueing up to be in line to get the full effect of his flippant entrance.

All the way back he would cudgel his brain for a new phrase, a cloak-flourishing raffish expression that Cosgrove of the *Daily Mail* would pilfer to top up his daily report on the Bomber Command.

A dozen of his choicest quips had aready found their way

into the most up-to-date glossaries of RAF slanguage, and were being tongued by pin-feathered cadets from John o' Groats to Melbourne.

Of course they had to get back. It had come to him, as it always did when things seemed particularly mucky. A five-shilling line, this one. Old Dyce had come through again.

"A main-event show," he decided he would say. "Straddled the toy shop beautifully. Quite a piece of cake, as raids go." Oh, there was no doubt about it, they simply had to get back. Old Cosgrove would love that one.

Jerry was planting diversion fires well to the west between Rathenow and Neustadt, hoping he could kid them into unloading their stuff before they reached Berlin. That was an old gag, but Dickie was certain of his new navigation instrument and he was positive of his position within a quarter of a mile. He racked his instruments, slipped away his book of navigation tables, and called Hammersley.

"About ten minutes to go, Skipper. I'll check drift again and set out the showcase, eh?"

"This is where they're holding the party!" Hammersley added over the intercom. "Gunners at the Alert! All stations report!"

The Wellingtons had stirred the gruel to the boiling point by now. Flak was screeching about the sky and the searchlights were piling an illuminated game of pick-up sticks. The moon was positively wizard and the Stirling shouldered her great mass through the simooms of concussion.

Michael Jobbins maintained his vigil in the dorsal turret. He reported through to Hammersley as he watched the rapier blades of the searchlights prod the sable sky and then suddenly slash and cut as if they would trim the uneven edges of the flame curtain being hung by the bombers ahead.

"It's all very gaudy," Jobbins commented, "but it don't com-pare with our shows. Not like that Guy Fawkes night when I

was going through 'Oundsditch. Ours was more even and regular.
We don't dab the blasted searchlights all over the playce, messin'
up the design, like. Our chaps seem to do it smoother and get on
with less bother. Like following a good draw at bowls."

That reflection made Jobbins sit up suddenly. He kicked the
traversing pedal and his guns swung around with an oily sigh.
He blinked twice, cocked his head to one side to encourage deeper
reflection, and then suffered the impact of realization that
smacked home with the thud of a howitzer buffer.

"Cor!" he gushed, like something spurting out of a punctured
tin lid. "We can't do any messing about tonight. I've got to
get back! We're meeting the 4th Armored Division at Kettering
tomorrow! The Air Commodore won't 'arf carry on if I ain't
there!"

He went limp under the awesome possibilities of the station
bowls team going to Kettering without him. Jobbins had been
honored with the important post of skip on the Air Commodore's
bowls team, the one recreational risk the portly station commander ventured. There were some degenerates who went about
mumbling that the Air Commodore would rather win a game
of lawn bowls than get into the King's birthday honors list.

"We've got to get back this time," Sergeant Jobbins muttered.
"Ooo-er! 'Ere's another one of the blighters!"

His guns swung back, elevated a trifle, and he let a Heinkel
night fighter have it smack in the engine cowling.

Aft, beyond the great halberd blade of fin and rudder,
Montague-Bates also took up the offensive. He had four guns
in his turret and Monty caught the Heinkel just as she reached
the dead stall point at the top of her screaming zoom. The distance was perfect and Monty brought her well inside the inner
ring of the sight and slapped a six-second burst that pickled her
properly.

"What the hell's going on back there?" Hammersley raged
over the intercom.

From his action station Dyce took full credit with: "My mob has just snaffled a Heinkel! We're wizard tonight, what?"

"Bomb doors open, Skipper!" Dickie Steadman reported from the bomb-sight platform. "Give me a run-up southeast to north-west, will you?"

"Descending to attack level," the pilot answered. "Action stations, Dyce. No messing about now. I've got to get back tonight!"

Jobbins cocked his ear at the intercom speaker and wondered whether they had eighteen-foot or twenty-one-foot rinks at Kettering.

"*You've* got to get back?" Macklin Montague-Bates queried amid the tangle of the tail turret. "What about me?"

Hammersley was slinging her through the bolsters of con-cussion and the dazzle of bale fire like a man possessed. The stub-winged Stirling answered his demands with reckless gaiety and Steadman had to spread his legs and elbows to stay on the pad. The drumfire from below crashed and erupted to mark their course with flame-splashed milestones.

Montague-Bates huddled behind his gun breeches aft of the fanning rudder and stared into the graph-streaked night. He was a small chap with delicate features that displayed the pinch of pecunious piety. His eyes flickered like a gutting studio lamp, his shoulders sloped under the bulky Sidcot suit that encumbered his dread-numbed frame. He constantly talked aloud to himself and used theatrical gestures to bring home his own points.

The turret was tilted high now, for the Stirling was nosing down at the target area below. Through the open bomb doors the slip stream wailed and sent a storm of dust and loose instru-ment covers against the battery of flame floats and reconnais-sance flares on the wall racks. Monty hung on to the cross members and wondered how long it would be before they hit smack in the middle of the devouring maw of flame and saw-toothed roofs below. Sergeant Bollinger had left his panel and taken his emergency post in the nose turret and was pouring a double stream into the grouping of gasometers huddled in the shadows that danced beyond the glare of the incendiaries.

This was the minute Monty dreaded. He felt entirely alone and helpless, trapped in a tangled environment, remote and apart. There was no one to talk to, no one to look at, no one who by glance or grimace could let him know what was taking place. The intercom offered only a mad, unintelligible jumble of cries, curses, commands, and confusion; the words and metallic raspings of the speaker vibrators intensified the realization that he had to get back this night of all nights.

He consulted his watch and made a quick calculation. Fully three hours had passed and there were three more to go. He figured again and the pile-up of hours made him gag on his dread.

"I put it on at seven thirty after the final briefing," he tongue-lashed himself again. "If I hadn't stopped to talk to that girl outside the N.A.A.F.I. hut ... It wouldn't have mattered. I've only got about fifty-five hours left!"

Hammersley brought the ship around again after the run-up and took the orders from Steadman. "Right, Skipper. Hold her due southeast now. Three thousand. I'd like to begin where the railway lines come out of the goods yard."

The pilot stiffened everything and waited until the compass card came around and then leveled her off for the actual attack.

"Right! Right, Skipper. Hold her on ... steady now ... there!"

The big Stirling jerked with the release of the load. Glued to his Wimperis sight, Steadman began to count and punch the release buttons in pairs. The bomb gear grumbled and the steadying springs scraunched as the eggs plunged away. Hammersley fought the big wheel and held her true while Kegworth peered out the side window and tried to determine the results.

Behind them on the fight-control platform Dyce stood anxiously waiting until the wing-cell bombs had cleared. He sucked in his breath and saw the guns of the dorsal turret swinging around.

"Bandits attacking from starboard quarter!" he bellowed into the intercom mike. "Get that swine, Monty!"

"Bombs away!" Steadman bellowed. "Bombs . . ."

The chorus of angry explosive roared below as Hammersley tilted the big plane over and shot through the searchlight glare. A rage of machine-gun metal slashed and cut through the dural walls of the fuselage and Hammersley let out a choked scream and threw his gloved hands to his face. The big wheel went wild and Kegworth hurled himself across the cockpit and grabbed at it. He gripped it tight, threw one arm across Hammersley's chest and held him clear.

"Bomb doors closed!" Steadman yelled.

Another glare of scarlet frenzy seared the sky and Dyce cried out, "Another Mess-up, Skipper! A proper flamer, that!"

The Stirling slithered into a quaking sideslip while Kegworth bellowed for assistance. "Dyce! Dyce! Give me a hand. Hammersley's stopped a creaser!"

There was a peal of exultation in Kegworth's voice even though the bomber had slobbered away several hundred feet of important altitude. The copilot dragged her out and got her nose level again while Hammersley floundered about trying to clear his Sutton straps and get away from the bank of white-knobbed throttles.

"Stopped a beauty, sir," assured Sergeant Bollinger as he came back and helped Dyce get Hammersley to the rest bunk. " 'E'll 'ave a narsty 'eadache in the mornin', but it's a real 'oliday tap."

"This one's worth ten quid," Dyce agreed as he pawed through the first-aid kit. "Some blokes have all the luck. You'll have to part your hair on the other side for a time. Now hold still and we'll have you ready for nursie by the time we get back."

"I'll contact the station, sir. They'll be all ready for you."

Kegworth cleared the big bomber and called for a position.

Jobbins and Montague-Bates were still packing it to the Mess-ups, like a couple of demons.

There was a distinct spasm of surrender that seemed to stop the bomber dead, and Kegworth screamed something from up front. Dyce stood erect, listened, and glanced out of a port.

"Tankage!" he yelled. " 'Struth! That's me!"

He raced forward and lurched to the engineer's panel and twisted a small black knurled wheel and snapped in a new series of fuel tanks. Kegworth held the bomber in a glide and methodically brought the two fluttering engines on the port side to a new bellow of triumph.

"Good! Good old Dyce!" he yelled.

"What's up?" Steadman demanded as he came up the catwalk. "Where's the Skipper?"

"Gone aft to have his hair finger-waved. He just stopped a beauty," said Dyce, delighted with his retort. They could always rely on old Dyce.

"Ooo-er!" bleated Steadman, making his way back to Kegworth. "Well in the clear now, Jimmie. Try it for half an hour on approximately three. That should take us north of the coast flak for a time at least. Sure you're all right?"

"Don't worry. I'll get her back. I've *got* to get back!"

"So have I. I've just discovered I can get a fix in about . . . But never mind. I'll finish up below and then come back and sit with you. Those blasted props out there bother me."

"Righto! Gunners report, please," Jimmie called, all aglow with the importance of his new command.

"All clear 'ere, sir," Jobbins answered. "We are a-goin' to get back all right, ain't we, sir? Me and Monty 'ave driven them off all right, sir."

"What do you say, Monty?" Jimmie demanded.

"I'm all right, sir. They seem to have bunged off after the others. We're going to get back all right, aren't we?" he pleaded.

"You can put next week's pay on Mr. Kegworth," Jimmie confided over the intercom. "Don't worry, lads. I've *got* to get back. It's something to do about a lady who's going to have a baby—several babies, in fact."

Greasy Neale slammed on through the night.

They touched in with just over six hours on the engine logs and Kegworth dabbed her down as gently as his enthusiasm and anxiety would permit. He rolled her up to her dispersal area, bellowing out of the slide hatch for Crockett.

Steadman clambered out first, holding his new instrument and explaining it to a bewildered Bollinger. "You see, I have this pair of mirrors which, combined with this prism, deflect the light of two particular stars into this telescope in such a manner that when the images are seen superimposed in the center of the field of view . . ."

"It's a bit too much for me, sir. I can do things wiv mirrors, like making a box of cigars disappear—but this sort of thing. By the way, sir, I 'opes you'll pop in and do the N.A.A.F.I. concert party tomorrow night," the Brilliant Bollinger said evasively.

Dyce and Jobbins appeared in the doorway, supporting Hammersley. The gunner saw that Steadman had grabbed the Air Commodore's attention. He hoped he'd get the chance to mention that he was back all right and would be available for the Kettering match.

"Here we are. Safe and sound," Dyce was saying. "You'll get at least two weeks in dock with this lot—and then a spot of leave, you lucky dog!"

But Flight Lieutenant Hammersley could only hold his head and curse his luck.

"Don't worry! Don't worry," the Air Commodore said with sympathy, and shoved Steadman and his new sextant to one side. "You can do with a rest. You'll have a squadron to worry about after this. Promotion, my boy! Everybody else all right?"

"All right?" Dyce crowed brazenly. "We shed a spot of Britain's bravest and bluest, sir; but it was a main-event show.

We straddled the toy shop beautifully! Quite a piece of cake, as raids go."

"Oh, good! Jolly good, that!" The Air Commodore beamed. Then he turned and made a grab for the gunner. "Here! Here, you. Where are you off to?"

It was Macklin Montague-Bates, all gear and gasps. Monty turned and fingered his crotch straps. He glanced at his wrist watch anxiously. "Me, sir? I've got to be off. You see, sir, I left my little wireless set on when we left, and it's a battery model—and there's only about fifty-five hours of juice left. I'll be back in a minute."

The Air Commodore just blinked.

Bataan Landing

CORPORAL PETE COYNE draws his pay regularly as a member of Number 4 Observation Squadron—most of it used to be squandered in the jitney creeps of Manila for refreshment and visual entertainment. Coyne is one of those dog-wagon warriors, and if Number 4 ever gets out of Corregidor and goes into reserve somewhere in Alaska, his first demand will be: "Gimme me a coke an' a hamboiger!"

The war had not made a great deal of difference to Pete. Of course, it had plummeted him into the unwelcome responsibility of a blitzkrieg rating, but he had company—the colonel had been a captain only three weeks before.

Coyne had been massaging the gears of a White half-track when the Japs began dumping five-hundred-pounders into Manila. The boost in pay provided a little extra pocket lettuce to spend on enlarging his informal education, and the transfer to the gun turret of one of their few remaining O-47's gave him the opportunity to try out some of the theories he had evolved from a close study of air adventure as presented in that classic volume *Aces Wild*.

The equipment line-up at Kindley Field was about as impressive as a rube air carnival—what material was left had been dispersed amid the shell craters and spread out under the apitong trees and abaca palms to prevent the Japs from slugging them.

Corporal Coyne was standing by in the shadow of Number 14's port wing. The heat of the afternoon swept across the jagged chunk of volcanic rock jutting out of the waters of Manila Bay, it came down through the tropical overlay of deep green jungle that quilts Corregidor's gray cliffs, and swirled up the dust of the runway and diffused the metal gleam of the three-place observation planes.

Pete ignored the discomfort. He squatted on a rigger's tool chest with his knobby knees locked together and his squirrel eyes devouring the glorious details of a certain Lieutenant Hank Scott's adventure against the Huns somewhere over the Wipers Canal.

"*Scott tooled his S.E.-5 into position,*" the author had penned. "*The Fokkers were preparing to slam down on the sluggish Limey crate below. The Harry Tate was cold meat unless Scott got there in time. He rammed the spade-grip forward and stood on the rudder bar as the single-seater dived dead on the gaudy Fokker that led the death-pack below. Scott pressed the button, and his guns yammered . . .*"

"Come on! Come on!" a voice yammered above the crash of *Hank Scott's* guns. "We gotter get ridin'!"

"Sure! Yes, sir!" Coyne spluttered and hastily stuffed the book into his back pocket. "Be right there!"

A three-place observation ship can provide more trouble than the eternal triangle. The pilot, Lieutenant Malcolm Breeze, gloried in his post—his sole idea of winning the war was to shoot at anything and everything. Lieutenant Stacy Sewell, his observer, had been an air-traffic man and displayed about as much flexibility of thought and action as one might expect to find in a Pan-Central Air Line timetable. Against these two fate had stacked Corporal Coyne, a romantic if there ever was one.

"Don't you get enough without gorging on that ancient history?" Breeze snorted at him.

"It ain't so ancient," Pete defended. "That's only the last war. Them guys really did a job!"

"How do you know?"

"It says so, here in the book. Them little scouts sure used to pack it to them Fokkers. That was some war, I guess."

"The way those rags write it up, it sure was. Wait till they get through with this one—you won't recognize it."

"But this is straight stuff, sir," Corporal Coyne attempted to argue.

"Let me tell you something, Coyne," Lieutenant Sewell broke in as he lumbered up with his load of operational gear and piled it under the fuselage stirrup. "There's more phony stuff in that old war dope than you can shake a stick at. I know. I've checked it. You put a slide rule on it, and none of it checks."

"Slide rule, Lieutenant?" Pete's face curdled into a dull blotch.

"Those guys diving through zeppelins!" the observer snorted. "Hitting balloon cables to destroy spotting kites! The one about the gunner who was tossed out of an old D.H.-4 and was caught again by the pilot before he hit the ground. They can't do it, Coyne! You can't beat facts and figures. No guy ever flew through a dirigible!"

Coyne was in no position to make his superiors appear ignorant, so he muffled his protestations with his chin piece and snapped the thigh straps of his parachute pack with dull interior rumblings.

"Come on," Breeze ranted. "Let's get on with the war. I got to get me a Mitsubishi. You guys and your arguments."

"There isn't any argument," proclaimed Sewell. "You can't argue with facts and figures. That's what's wrong with this war—too many people trying to be heroes, and not enough straight figuring."

"Maybe that's what's wrong with MacArthur," Breeze taunted with a sly grimace.

"The only thing the matter with General MacArthur is that he's ignorant of certain facts. That's why we're being sent out again. I'm supposed to find out where the Japs have a secret landing ground. You think of nothing but shooting down planes. Coyne is figuring out how he can become a hero by the standards set in that fool book. I'm the only guy who is acting sane."

"Do the Japs have any dirigibles for us to dive through?" asked Breeze in mock seriousness.

"It isn't the spectacular efforts of the grandstanding few who will win this war," said Sewell with a patronizing air. "Knowledge is power. That's why they train us observers."

"It wouldn't be because you flunked out on primary aerobatics at Randolph, would it?"

"Any dope can fly a plane! Even Coyne could be taught that much."

"Yeh?" Pete muttered as he scrambled up the side of the O-47. "You wait, Mr. Sewell. Lots of swell war pilots began as gunners. There was McCudden, and Bishop . . ."

Number 14 creaked as the crew climbed in; Breeze took the forward seat and kicked in the starter; Sewell, all biff and pencils, was accommodated under the direction-finder ring where he assumed his air of important business; Coyne had to be content with the poor arrangements aft, where he hoped to furnish some measure of defense with a single Browning gun.

The Cyclone engine boomed out and growled at the scream of shells that were coming out of the rifles at Fort Drum and burying their ringed snouts deep in the sands along the Pilar Road.

The Intelligence captain came out of the underground quarters waving a sheet of paper, so Sewell shoved back the hatch cover and leaned out into the prop stream as the two-bar guy barked further orders into his earpiece: "The colonel thinks maybe you have something on this landing-strip idea. There's a hint of camouflage there. He wants you to get another shot at it from about twenty-five hundred, at forty-five degrees."

"Can do!" Sewell agreed with a triumphant gleam.

"We carrying that cockpit camera again?" grumbled Breeze over the radio-panel bulkhead. He gave the Cyclone the octane, and Number 14 rumbled down what was left of Kindley Field. The dust swept up, rolled itself into a huge ball and descended on the .50-caliber ack-ack emplacement. Breeze drew her off carefully, swung over into a tight climbing turn that would have netted him twenty gigs at Randolph Field, and brought her out over the garrulous waters of lower Manila Bay.

The 75-mm. guns tucked away in the jungle area of Bataan pumped out a warning bracket on a speck flashing toward Malolos. Pete Coyne studied the signal and began to fidget with the slide-away gun mounting.

"Take it easy, von Richthofen," Sewell sneered. "It's only a Jap Nakajima. She'll stay there as long as those Gyrines keep shooting. I got to get pictures. Never mind your running up a score!"

"Yes, sir!" Pete nodded.

"Cut back for the east shore," Sewell ordered over the cockpit communication set. "We'll work up from there and follow the road across to Olongapo and down again to Bagac."

"What about that guy the Marines are checking up there?"

"Leave him for the fighters. We're getting pictures."

"What fighters?" Breeze argued. "If we dump those guys, the landing strip won't matter, will it?"

"You been reading a book, too?" snorted Sewell.

The sore thumb of Bataan was blotched with shell scars. The road along the east shore was barricaded with felled timber. Gashes hacked out of the apitong and nipa palm suggested gun positions, and scorched vegetation marked where MacArthur's gunners had fired point-blank over open sights into charging waves of Japanese troops as they stormed across the beaches and sought a toe hold.

Breeze circled south of Pilar and waited until Sewell caught the strip and semaphore signals and had charted the new line positions for the squadron map back at Corregidor.

"They're holding on," Sewell muttered. "I don't know how they do it. They were supposed to have been clamshelled out of there ten days ago."

"Maybe MacArthur ain't seen the facts and figures yet," suggested Breeze in dumb monotone.

"Okay. You have your fun with words, but how about getting some work done?"

"Boy, I wish we were over the Burma Road." Breeze leveled the O-47 off and headed north. He wished Sewell wouldn't flaunt his devotion to duty so much. He resented being encumbered with two yard birds like Sewell and Coyne. Sewell was bad enough, but Coyne was the prize dope of the first pressing—Coyne and his book!

"Where you heading?" Sewell jerked him out of his train of thought. "You'll be relieving Singapore unless you snap out of that stupor."

The pilot saw he had passed well beyond Hermosa and was dead over the road that leads northeast to San Fernando. The Jap guns were blasting away again, their dirty-white puffballs setting up rough Southern Cross insignia four hundred feet below. The thud of concussion blasted all about them, and the sluggish observation plane lurched lackadaisically in the uneven swell and seemed to be stifling a yawn.

"If you fly straight across, holding a course on the upper end of Subic Bay," Sewell suggested, "I might be able to get a line on that area again."

Breeze argued, "All I've seen here is jungle and rocks. You couldn't put an open umbrella down in there."

"When you're trained in observation," Sewell taunted, "you learn to put two and two together. You don't have to believe anything until you have proved it to yourself."

"You mean to tell me..." Breeze began, but Sewell shut him off with further attention to the radio panel.

Breeze bridled, but then tightened up. "Maybe you're right," he yelled into his muzzle mike. He had spotted a gray Karigane two-seater below, blotched in against the gaudy verdure of bamboo palm, guijo trees, and abaca fronds. The nose of the O-47 went down with a lunge.

Sewell tried to head off the pilot, but he was helpless behind the radio panel. Coyne began rattling his artillery again, but

Sewell slapped him across the shoulders. "You stay put! Cover
our tail. We're being sucked in!"

"This is the way it should be." Coyne grinned. "Just like
you read . . ." The pilot was high tailing down so fast Pete was
unable to punch out the words; the slip stream sliced his breath
away.

The gunner aboard the Karigane saw them in plenty of time;
Jap three-inchers rifled opposition long before Breeze was anywhere within range, and chunks of Kobe shell pelted through
the fuselage and cut Wailing Winnies in the skin.

"You damned fool!" Sewell yelled.

But Breeze was on his way to glory, his sight stick lanced
dead at the fishtailing Karigane, while the Jap gunner poured
it back at them.

"Lieutenant Breeze got the right idea," Corporal Coyne reflected.

Breeze pumped a few short bursts, the tracer streaked across
the sky and drew chalky lines between the two war planes. He
held her steady, but there was a damper of air pressure billowing up from the heated hills and the O-47 bucked like a stal-
lion. It was like trying to draw a bead from the front seat of a
roller coaster.

The heavy O-47 almost scraped her belly over the Jap's cockpit
covers before Breeze sensed he had missed. With visions of the
Order of the Rising Sun, Third Class, the Karigane tossed with
his gods and pressed the trigger of his Nambu gun; the 6.5 slugs
stitched a wicked line of perforation along the muck-streaked
belly of the O-47. The motor retched and coughed as Breeze
drew her out of her headlong plunge—a lifetime of hope and
fear was compressed into the next ten seconds.

"What the—" Breeze gurgled as he stared about with his
mouth wide open. Sewell finished it for him: "You damned fool!
You took all he had—cold! I told you!"

They sat constricted and trembled in sympathy with the

frantic gasps of the motor. The pilot punched at various adjustments on the Chandler-Groves in a hopeless effort to get her to take it up again. The prop churned over with the sluggish ambition of a dilapidated windmill and ground up enough loose metal to provide a suitable nerve-shredding accompaniment.

Coyne, who had no idea of what had actually happened, reacted normally. He whipped out the Browning again and blasted off a four-second burst at the Jap two-seater below and torched her tanks as she tried to edge around for a front-gun attack.

"That lug was tryin' to get a burst into us!" Pete bawled, and then realized the adventure was jumping the cogs and getting out of the groove.

In the confined cockpit the three men gripped objects that were most familiar; Coyne blinked and clutched the grips of the Browning; Sewell held the ends of his radio panel, his mouth would not form the words he was trying to scream; Breeze clawed at the control column as though he would throttle it for even suggesting there was nothing left.

"We're going—down!" finally spurted out of Sewell. "We're going down—prisoners!"

Bewildered and unbalanced, Coyne again pressed the button of his gun and lashed .30-caliber stuff into the jungle below.

"Shut that damn thing off!"

Peter released the weapon and it hung disconsolately on the mounting. He sought an answer in the jagged outline of their shadow racing along against the green sea of tropical foliage.

"Stow that thing away!" Sewell yelled at him. "It'll crack your noggin!"

The gunner shoved it under the fuselage hump and as he was turning around, limp and resigned, the plane hit.

"Hang on!" Sewell started to yell, but he was slammed with a cruel thud against the radio panel, and Coyne catapulted forward against the cushion provided by the observer's body. The O-47 sliced the tops out of the palms and, with a scream of metal surging through her wings, plunged on to smash up at the base of a tree.

Pete shook himself free and muttered, "Nice of the lieutenant to tell me about the gun."

He crawled through the fracture in the hatch and waited for Sewell and Breeze to follow him.

"Lieutenant!" he called. His eyes straightened out and swept the wreck. "You can't stay there! We gotta get trackin'!"

He tottered about uncertainly, wondering what he was supposed to do next. He sniffed, caught the tang of gasoline, and an unprecedented sense of duty jetted through him. As Sewell's arms came over the edge of the hatch, Pete saw the painful twists of the hands; the observer's face, a mask of uneven planes and streaked with a fine tracery of scarlet, hooked its chin over the cover slide.

Pete climbed up again and dragged out a short ax and cut and slashed with tottering inaccuracy until he had a gash in the side through which he helped Sewell to crawl. The observer got to his feet and then stumbled drunkenly to a curved palm trunk and leaned there with his arms at grotesque angles.

"Both arms—when I braced myself against the panel," he babbled as he slid down the palm butt and rolled over.

"You stay there, sir," Pete suggested dubiously. "Wait till I get Lieutenant Breeze out."

From the jagged wing root the gunner hacked until he had gouged out another panel. The pilot was slumped over, his arms swinging between his splayed knees.

"You sure stopped som'pin, eh, Lieutenant?" Pete wailed.

He then dragged Breeze into the clear and scrambled through the nipa and fern until he had him on his back beside Sewell. There was a deep, grinning gash across the pilot's forehead and blood drooled across the undulations of his face.

Pete loosened the chin piece of the helmet and returned to the plane for the first-aid kit in the observer's locker. He then daubed and fumbled bluntly with gauze pads, bound the wads into place with bandage, and pulled Breeze's ear flaps down and strapped them.

He stripped off his coverall and parachute harness, tossed them aimlessly toward the wreck, and turned his attention to Sewell. Sympathetic reasoning and latent perspicacity dictated his efforts to help the observer. He placed Sewell's lower arms together with the gloved fists cupping the elbows, and bound them with what was left in the first-aid can. Strips of fabric ripped from the rudder completed a bulky but satisfactory support.

"The lieutenant says you can't do it," he muttered, "but *Lieutenant Scott* did it." He stared about him. Breeze was snorting unintelligibly and trying to get up.

"Take it easy, Lieutenant. You got nothin' to worry about."

Breeze struggled to one elbow. "That you—Coyne? Where's Sewell?" he asked thickly.

"Right there alongside you."

Pete watched him with tortured eyes as Breeze peered about.

"Where are you, Coyne?"

"Jees! I'm right here—kneelin' right in front of you."

The bandaged head came up again and stopped, its sponson of gauze trained on the gunner. "But—I can't see you—either of you. I can't see anything!"

"Maybe you got a lot of blood in your eyes."

"It—it isn't blood. I'm blind—blind! I can't see a thing! Holy God!"

Sewell drew up his legs and tried to peer into Breeze's face.

"You got a smack across the head, sir," Pete whimpered. "Maybe it's only just for now. Maybe you got such a headache you can't see, eh?"

"Where are we?" Breeze appealed in a half-whisper.

Coyne dropped to his knees again and crawled forward. He wondered if Breeze was really blind. He waited, watching intently, then he turned slowly toward Sewell. The observer's eyes confirmed the fear that was beating a trip-hammer warning in

Coyne's chest. He saw Sewell nod, and he lurched forward suddenly and snatched Breeze's automatic from the hip holster.

"Where are we, Coyne?" Breeze asked again, and then sensed what was happening. "Damn you, Coyne! Come back with that gun!"

Pete rolled away with the big automatic hugged to his belly.

"Why don't you shut up, Breeze?" Sewell hissed through his puffed lips. "The guy's just trying to make you comfortable."

Breeze lay flat on the tangled foliage and stared with sightless eyes at the marquee of palm fronds that swayed gently in the tropical air.

"Thanks. Thanks, Sewell," he sobbed. "Good scout, that guy Coyne. You all right?"

"Sure. I'm swell!"

Half an hour later Breeze struggled up to a sitting position. Sewell was still hunched at the butt of a big palm watching the pilot. "Take it easy," he muttered quietly.

"Where's Coyne?"

"I don't know. He went off, scouting around to see where we are. He'll be back. Thinks he knows this area. Says he drove a half-track on maneuvers here last summer."

"The dopey guy might get away with it yet," Breeze said tonelessly. "God, I wish I could see!"

"Don't worry—you will. You got a smack that gave you an anemic reaction as the result of loss of blood. It's just temporary," Sewell said slowly and thoughtfully.

"Jees! Old facts and figures again. For once I hope you're right."

"They got a lot of that in the other war—temporary blindness."

"You got it figured out now that no one was really blinded, eh?"

"Listen! Here he comes," Sewell warned, "or someone, anyway."

A sweaty figure emerged from the tangle of vines that walled them in. It was Coyne, panting and beaming. "You wuz right,

Lieutenant!" he yelled at Sewell. "They got a strip back there—
about a quarter of a mile. Planes and trucks lined up. It's blocked
out with curtain camouflage."

"I'm not goin' to lay here and rot in this jungle," Breeze
growled.

"We can get there in half an hour," Pete continued. "It will
be almost dark then. We can torch this wreck, and they'll all
come to find out where we hit."

"Where the devil did you read that?" Sewell demanded.

"That's the book again, and maybe Pete has something."

He helped them to their feet with rough enthusiasm. "Anyway, we should burn her, shouldn't we?" he suggested, and
fingered for a match. He crossed to the tangle of fuselage, tore
open his parachute pack, and stuffed the billowing wad of silk
inside the pilot's cockpit. He applied the match and stepped
back to watch the flames lick up and eat away the fuel lines
that fed the carburetor.

"I don't know why he doesn't have an idea to stick on the
wings again and slingshot us off a bamboo tree," Sewell muttered as the flames roared up.

"You wait. I'll bet he's got an idea that has that one beat a
mile," Breeze husked as he swayed drunkenly.

"You better keep your packs, eh?" Pete suggested as he came
up and took their arms. "They'll be nice for you to sit on, if
we get a lift."

As they made their way through the spiny thicket, the hot
glare from the burning observation plane threw a gaudy orange-
tinted canopy at the sky. Coyne hacked a path and helped them
along. The observer walked wide-legged and stumbled now and
then, but he plunged on after the encouraging chatter of Coyne,
who dragged Breeze through the jungle ahead.

"It's only a little way now, Lieutenant," he said as he steadied
the blind pilot. "Listen! You can hear them scrambling through,

over there toward the fire. You still got that headache, Lieutenant?"

"I got one that will last for fifty years," Breeze mumbled with
his head bent over.

"Maybe we can git some aspirin."

The route was tortuous and winding and it seemed an hour
before they came into a clearing. Breeze could hear the metallic
activity, and Sewell could see what he had long suspected. The
landing strip had been cut through the sparse area of vegetation, and from a series of bamboo poles set along the sides
dangled shallow curtains of net and light cloth on which tufts
of dry grass, palm leaves, and sprays of ferns had been laced.

"Baby! They can keep pounding our guys for twenty-four
hours a day from this hole!" Sewell gasped.

On one side was a collection of trucks, fuel wagons, and light
tanks; on the near side, their tails drawn into hacked-out dispersal
areas, stood several indistinct planes. Vague figures moved in and
out of the lights flickering from small portable tanks.

"What are we waiting for?" Breeze whispered.

"I remember this spot," Pete added. "We used it for a transport
park. Maybe we could swipe a truck."

"That's out," Sewell said from a shadow. "There's no road
out of here going south."

"That's what I was going to say, sir. The only way out..."

"Here we go," Sewell moaned.

"What's he got to lose?" Breeze demanded, as he moved about
aimlessly. "I'm willing to go with the guy!"

"Who's going to fly it?" Sewell argued uncertainly. "You—well,
you can't see right now, and I got two busted arms. Coyne
can't fly."

"Two busted arms?" Breeze sucked in his breath. "But you
said you were... Then Coyne *has* to...."

"Listen!" Pete whispered. "They're runnin' one up—right
down our alley. Maybe if we got aboard, Lieutenant Breeze

could get it off—blind, an' we could tell him where to head it."

"Sure!" Breeze added. "All we got to do is get it into the air. We can pile it up anywhere on the other side."

The enthusiasm of illogical thinking beat down any sane view of the situation. For one thing, it was obvious that the blazing observation plane had drawn many of the ground crew from their posts.

Uncertain, but unwilling to be left behind, Sewell followed Coyne and Breeze through the shadows.

"It's one of their Kariganes, sir," Pete confided to Breeze as he led him along. "We can all get aboard, eh?"

"Be a tight squeeze. Which way is she headed?"

"Across the runway. If we can get those Japs out of the way, it will be easy."

"How many guys around her?"

"I can see only two. One in the cockpit, runnin' her up."

"O.K. You get those guys out of there. We'll stay here."

The first Jap was easy. He was bending over the tail, holding it down while the mechanic in the cockpit tested the A-14 motor. A solid smack with the gun butt of the automatic Pete had taken from Breeze brought the Jap to his knees and he rolled over with a grunt.

"An' *stay* there!" Pete growled as he dragged him clear.

Then he moved like a cat to the wing root and climbed up. The puzzled Jap mechanic stared into Pete's gun tunnel and started to shut off the motor. "No! No! Let her rumble," Pete ordered. "You just get out and give *me* a hand."

Exaggerated gestures with the gun clearly interpreted his meaning. Now a suety gray, the Jap stumbled down off the wing root in feverish haste, but Coyne collared him and rammed him toward the tail.

"Lift!" he explained with his hands. "You lift while I push—compree?"

"Take my arm," Sewell whispered. "Grab me under the arm-pit—easy. That mug is going to get away with it."

"All the facts and figures are against it, aren't they?" Breeze said with a smirk in his voice. "If I could only see!"

Coyne had the Karigane out and turned around, as Sewell and Breeze reached the wing tip. The pilot felt his way along the trailing edge and was clambering up when another businesslike *thock* thudded somewhere in the darkness.

"An' *stay* there!" Coyne repeated as the Jap mechanic cork-screwed to the ground.

He came up to the fuselage, grinning. "I guess Lieutenant Sewell had better take the back seat. I'll stand between you—somehow. Get in, sir. The throttle's on the left side, just like ours. You're headed straight down the runway."

Breeze fumbled about and instinctively his hands found the control column and the throttle; his feet slid forward and rested on the rudder pedals, which he waggled experimentally.

"She'll fly like a Mack truck," he grumbled.

"Get going, Lieutenant. Here comes a mob over from them trucks. You're dead center down the runway."

"Hey! Wait a minute!" Sewell yelled, as he tried to lean forward. "How the hell we going to get this thing down again?"

"You can step out if you like," Breeze growled.

"Sure. We can, but Coyne..."

The rest was drowned out when Breeze eased the throttle up the gate; the 800-hp radial picked it up smartly and she began to rumble down the runway.

"Steady, Lieutenant," Pete instructed. "You're bearing a bit right—and don't take her off too soon, or you'll hit the curtain camouflage. Left, sir—*left!*"

"Just like a Mack truck!" Breeze growled over his chin piece.

"*Left,* sir! You're gonna take her wing tip off!"

The pilot rammed his buttocks down hard and pressed the left rudder. She was trying to clear by herself now. He eased the column forward and felt the wheels thump off the uneven

track. Her tail was up and she answered the rudder reasonably
fast.

"Good! Hold her now. Hold her down, sir. We got a few
more yards to clear."

"Listen, you dopes," Sewell was yelling behind Pete's back.
"How we going to get down?"

"Take her away, sir. You're in the clear!" Pete turned in
triumph to yell at Sewell, who was jabbing him with his knee.
"We got away wid a enemy plane—an' escaped!"

Sewell glared at him in frank disgust. "Sure. We stole an
enemy plane. Now figure out how you're going to get it down
again. I get two broken legs now, I suppose."

Breeze took the Karigane over the palm barrier with amazing
ease. A trickle of tracer crept up from the area where the
transport had been parked; ahead, over the knobby nose of
Santa Rosa crater, the Bataan line was jeweled with serried gashes
of gunfire and the sparkle of signal rockets.

Coyne squatted behind the bucket seat that encased Breeze's
back and peered forward for the outline of Mount Bataan. A
welter of disjointed thoughts doused the first warm blaze of
enthusiasm of having effected an escape.

"You're heading straight down the peninsula, sir," he advised
the pilot. "We should be getting some of our own fire soon."

Breeze nodded with resignation. "Can't be helped. Keep me
well clear of that crater and then turn me right so that we go
past Bataan and out to sea. I'll circle that, and approach Corregidor from the west. That should evade a lot of it—until
we get in."

"Sure! Then once you get over the island, you and Lieutenant
Sewell kin take to the silk. I'll stay and see if I can get her down."

"You're nuts! You'd splatter yourself all over the island."

"What are we going to do?" the trussed-up Sewell yelled
from the rear.

"You got about fifteen miles to figure it out," Breeze barked.
"Two of us have chutes, one guy burned his up. I might be

able to set this thing down if Coyne could read the instruments for me."

"Some are in American and some in Japanese," Pete said after a glance over the instrument board. "Turn sharp right now, sir."

"Ninety degrees?"

"Sharp right—I don't know how many. . . . There! Now get her straight again. You'll soon be through the two peaks."

"You're through," Sewell said. "Now turn left—ninety, and you'll be heading south down the beach. The island is just around the bend."

After another five minutes of flight Breeze asked, "Where are the flaps, Coyne? We should be somewhere by now."

The gunner leaned over and felt around below the pilot's knees. "They's a hand wheel on this side, sir."

"Oke! I'll give her a twist or two and see what happens."

The wheel proved to be the flap control and the Karigane snubbed into a slower speed on the brake pressure and Breeze drew back the throttle until the engine was only just ticking over.

"You're only about four miles away now, Lieutenant," Pete almost whispered over Breeze's shoulder.

"Oke! Keep me dead on. When we get within a quarter of a mile of the western end, let me know and I'll run across Kindley and we'll see what happens."

The Corregidor searchlights blazed out and fingered into the cumulus.

"What's that?" Breeze said suddenly, sitting upright. A shell arced up from the island fortress and spoke its wrath fifty feet below their port wing tip.

"That's our guns, sir. They got the searchlights out, too," Pete explained.

Sewell edged forward and tried to see around Coyne. He felt himself relax, and he sensed that Coyne *was* going to get away with something.

The Karigane slipped into the long glide with sluggish movements of the wing tips. Another searchlight slapped out from

Fort Drum and bathed the Jap plane in swabs of garish silver.
The three-inchers from Fort Hughes spanked the course with
convulsive gashes in the backdrop of the night.

"I wouldn't waste too much time here," Sewell advised. "You'd
better hit the channel between Corregidor and Caballo. If you
make a 120-degree turn to the left there, you'll be heading
straight down the long runway—if we make it."

For some reason Breeze didn't answer.

"I got it figured out, Lieutenant," Coyne rattled on. "We're at
fourteen hunnerd, over the channel now. You bring her around,
like he said, an' I'll try to help you in."

"Sure. Any dope can fly a plane. They almost taught Sewell
once," Breeze answered. "When we get around and headed for
the runway, you lean over, Pete, and put your hand on mine.
I'll fly her by the seat of my pants, and you can ease her off
when we look like we're going to sock the wheels down."

Coyne beamed. "I'll bet you, I—we—can get her down!"

"I'll bet you can," muttered Sewell with a numb grin.

"Don't let me slow her up to less than seventy. I don't want
to spin her in."

Breeze sat steady, his head held in the unnatural tension of a
blind man, but under his wad of bandage he was smiling. "Are
we still dead on, Coyne?"

"Dead on, Lieutenant. Hold her there."

"You put your hand on top of mine. She's yours, Corp."

The guns from Corregidor blasted at them with furious ambition and the searchlights crisscrossed and attempted to snip them
in two with their great silver blades. Coyne hugged close to the
pilot's shoulder and breathed the lateral directions.

"Right, gently. We're dead over the shore line now. Keep her
there, gently. The runway is dead ahead."

"Air speed, Coyne? What's our air speed?"

"Er—seventy-four. Left—just a trifle."

Sewell sat back, relaxed and complacent. He wondered how

long it took to mend two busted arms. He tried to see past Coyne's shoulder again, but the corporal was bobbing about and peering out of the cockpit windows.

"Down to sixty-eight, sir. Just skipping the main hangar. They ain't shooting now. Just looking up at us. Them dumb Gyrines!"

"Right! Take it, Coyne," Breeze ordered quietly. "Keep your hand on mine and ease her back—*ease* her back, when you see the runway racing under the leading edge."

The corporal wound his left arm around Breeze's chest, his right hand on top of the pilot's gloved fist, and jerked and pump-handled the control, but the pilot steadied him somehow. The Karigane ballooned off the pressure set up between the wing and the runway, and Breeze eased her back.

"Now! *Now*, sir!" Coyne gushed. "We're practically—"

The stick went back at the right instant, and her tail wheel touched, levering the front wheels down. The Karigane bounced once, and tried to ground-loop, but Breeze caught her with an aileron and a punch of rudder. She scraped to a stop.

"Nice flying, Coyne," Breeze said quietly. "I'll try to turn her and get her back to the hangar. You check me."

It took fully fifteen minutes to explain everything and get Breeze and Sewell off to the hospital bay. The medical officer kept saying, "It's nothing serious. Temporary blindness caused by the loss of blood and shock. Affects the optic nerves. Form of anemia which breaks down the blood picture. He'll be all right."

Sewell turned on his cot and looked at Breeze, who was flat on his back. The M.O. had gone out to do a check on Coyne.

"Nice going, Breeze," Sewell said quietly.

The pilot turned over slowly and winked. "When did you catch on?"

"When you jerked at the searchlight. I don't think Coyne knows. He thinks *he* landed that plane."

"Good! Don't ever tell him. He did me a very good turn back there."

"When he swiped your gun?"

"Yeh! I was pretty low then. I guess I did a job for him, eh?"

"Guys like Coyne," Sewell observed, "win wars, but they never know it—because of guys like you."

Assignment to Korea

FIELD ORDER 71 was a yard-long teletype strip that sent a depleted fighter group from an air base in Japan to a target nestled in some foothills thirty miles east of P'yŏng-yang, and gave Brian Corinth the best war story he'd ever filed for *Week-End Magazine*. That show opened what the boys later called Hell Week when they lost more F-80's than the Big Brass allowed should be mentioned. The murk over Seoul was nine tenths and the Weather Office in Tokyo could promise nothing better for nearly forty-eight hours.

"Sangkwong it is, then," the general said, and wished they'd fight a war where he could pronounce the names. "With concentration on that tank-repair park. Keep me posted on the weather."

Captain Bob MacLean was logging some sack time when Bill Pritchard, the public-relations officer, shook him and announced: "Hey, Mac! Here's a friend of yours. Rise and shine." He turned to the war correspondent and grinned. "There's your home-town hero. See you at dinner if you two ever get talked out."

MacLean cranked to his elbows and stared into the half-light of the gloomy hut. He may have been young and good-looking once, but he had seen too many long-range missions in the last two weeks.

"Hiya, Bob," the war correspondent half-whispered as he squatted on the corner of the black metal cot. "It's Corinth—Barney Corinth. Gwyn asked me to look you up. Shake out of it, pal."

Captain MacLean squinted through sleep-swollen eyelids, coughed, and palmed the oily fringe from his furrowed forehead. The squint gave him the expression of a sullen brigand, and in his initial haze he tried to connect Corinth with some target area. He remembered Warnemünde, Hamm, and places like the submarine pens at Saint-Nazaire. Corinth had to be in Greece. What the hell were they doing in Greece?

"Just four days ago I was dancing with Gwyn," the war correspondent rattled on. "Now I'm back at the old grind. Pop gave me a farewell party at the club, and Gwyn was there. Flew through yesterday. You remember me—eh, Mac?"

The sleepy airman ground out another hacking cough, closed one eye, and brought the speaker in more distinctly. "You were dancing with Gwyn? . . . Barney Corinth?" he inquired churlishly. "I don't get it. She didn't tell me."

"I was finishing up a script for Majestic Pictures when this mess breaks out and old Slater of *Week-End Magazine* asked me to pick up the assignment."

MacLean sat up peevishly and tossed the blanket clear. He zipped his pants and frowned at the neat, tidy man at the end of his bed.

"You saw Gwyn?"

"Just four days ago," Corinth repeated.

"You got yourself another war, eh?" MacLean was thinking it was pretty soft for these newspaper guys getting priority trips, circling around on the fringe of the wars, getting all the glory and hunks of currency, their names over the war stories they milked out of the poor devils who fought the wars for them. Back home they got all the dinners and dances at the country clubs. Maybe they got more—with other guys' wives and girls. He remembered this Corinth character from the last one. Son-of-a-brick had been everywhere and seen everything— to hear him tell it. He'd nested up a sweet spot for himself.

Outside, a jet opened up with a roar and began tearing long

strips of calico. "You saw Gwyn?" Mac repeated. He scowled and reached for a butt. "How'd that come about?"

"Like I said. Pop threw a party. Gwyn happened to be at the club on some Red Cross session and Pop hauled her in. I had a couple of dances with her and she asked me to look you up if I got out your way. She gave me your Group number, and all that."

A warm smile broke the harshness of MacLean's expression. "Hey, you saw Gwyn? How was she? How does she look?" The questions torrented out unrestrained. "I mean—what was she wearing? How's she taking it?"

"She—she looked fine, Mac. I only had a dance or two."

"What was she wearing? Give me a detailed picture, scribe. I always like her best in green—you know, with her copper hair and her eyes. She's all right, eh?"

Corinth looked puzzled. "I guess I didn't notice. She had on something smart—and nice. Gwyn always looks smart whatever she wears."

Mac doused his butt. Sure, this monkey wouldn't be looking at Gwyn's clothes; he'd have his eyes where there wasn't any. He was that sort of guy—too busy taking in the other features. Imagine not remembering whether she wore a green gown or a yellow cocktail dress!

"I got an air-mail letter this morning," he challenged. "She didn't mention you."

"She danced with a lot of guys," Corinth tried to explain.

MacLean pawed around for a towel and a soapbox. "Sure. Take it easy while I wash up."

Corinth waited; his mind in the briefing room. Command had the targets and aiming points lined up. They were figuring the routes in and out of Taejon, the bombing altitudes and radio procedure. Once more the teletypes were clattering, and outside the birds were tuning up for the evensong, and a creaky wheeled cart was hauling away the garbage.

A door at the opposite end of the hut burst open as the special-services officer came in and began packing up some gear on a bed three aisles away. He stuffed it carefully in a B-bag, wrote something on a shipping tag, and stacked it near the door. Corinth watched but didn't ask any questions. He knew that guys were being killed in this war, just the same as in the last. Guys weren't coming back from missions, and other guys were packing their bags for shipment.

MacLean came back with a slow, limp-kneed gait and began to fold his blankets. He still looked bushed in spite of the wash-up.

"So you're still in the writing racket?" He shoved a comb through his thick curly hair. "You never did get hooked for real duty, eh?"

Corinth colored. "I didn't wait for the draft in the last one. I volunteered, but the medics said no."

"Too much sugar in your water?"

Corinth wondered why all the gripe. "Nothing like that. Just enough to make me 4-F, but not bad enough to keep me out of Guadalcanal, Iwo Jima, and a few of those resorts."

"Sure. I know. I read some of your stuff once. You sure had a lot of luck, as I remember."

"All sorts of luck," Corinth admitted, and then brightened. "I figure there's a good story to you jet guys. Back home they got the idea jets aren't paying their keep. I figured you could give it to me straight."

"I'd like to get you a story," MacLean reflected bitterly to himself. "I'd like to show you what a jet has to do, buster. I'd like to take you over Korea and have you sweat one out—low down."

The correspondent was saying, "I mean, you guys aren't getting in the box score. They say you can't spend enough time over the area. Maybe when you get an air strip to work from in Korea?"

"Maybe you should find out for yourself," MacLean growled.

"I could fix you up. We got a T-33 two-seater jet here. It's used for check-out flights and Army observers. If you could stand a little altitude going over..."

"I've been on oxygen," Corinth caught himself saying. "Out in the Pacific—in the last shindy."

"You could get it straight—an eyewitness job," the jet Joe said, but was thinking: "This will be a party like you never saw in any California country club." He knew the layout of that club. The dining room had big french doors and it was simple to step out and wander down to the first tee. He'd heard a lot about that bench under the trees near Number 1.

"Maybe I could go—on a milk run," Corinth said hollowly.

"Milk run, hell! You can get that stuff from public-relations handouts."

"Pritchard said you were about through, Mac," the reporter parried. "I mean, your tour's about up." There was no percentage in going on a mission with a man who had used up most of his time. Mac was acting like a ghost clutching at something secure; as if he hoped a war correspondent would bring him some measure of luck. He'd had the same thing at Tarawa when he was with that infantry outfit. A war correspondent was supposed to be better than fighter cover when they hit a beach. Stuff like that.

"I got maybe four more—and I finish up." Mac kept his eyes on Barney. "Don't worry. I'll get you back."

Because Barney Corinth was endowed with one quality of fear that canceled out another, he said: "It's O.K. with me—if they'll let me go."

"Sure they'll let you go. The B-29's took some Judy on a bombing mission the other day." Mac's eyes were like polished stars. "You haven't seen a war until you've done a jet mission, keed!"

And Corinth added the snapper: "Yeh, I guess I should go.

Maybe when I get back home I could tell Gwyn what it was like. I know you heroes never open up."

Mac got that fast. Corinth had it all worked out. He even figured on going back and seeing Gwyn and telling her what a pushover jet missions were. Why not? It was a four-to-one bet in any book. If he gets back, I still have to make three more trips.

There was doubt in Captain Pritchard's gray eyes when Mac-Lean outlined his plan to take Corinth over to Korea in the two-seater job. The public-relations officer was long and lean and his thoughts moved in lagging advances, but he had been at his job long enough to assay most situations. "I don't like any part of it," he said as he tried to figure Mac's angle.

"He wants a real story on a jet strike," Mac argued with him. "If he goes on a trip, he'll see plenty."

"Maybe, but they won't let him write most of it. You know that."

"They won't be able to argue if the guy actually flies the mission," MacLean persisted.

"We've lost half-a-dozen correspondents already," Pritchard pointed out. "Suppose you get knocked down? Just suppose he stops a hunk of flak? What's in it for him, Mac? He's a civilian. His wife won't get any government insurance . . ."

"He hasn't got a wife! The guy's on his own." Mac reflected that Corinth could have his pick when he went back. He might even pick Gwyn. Mac didn't like any of that country-club business, because Barney didn't have a straight story on it. He couldn't even remember what Gwyn wore! He should have been able to see—if the lights were on.

"It might not be too bad," Corinth muttered. "I mean—going with a man like Mac who has had so much experience."

"This is Korea," the public-relations man reminded him. "Whatever he did in Europe is all behind him. Then he was on Mustangs. Today he's tooling a jet, and everything happens faster—and much lower down. These Kor-Reds have ack-ack stuff that makes Jerry's look like a putty blower."

"That's what he wants to see," MacLean stated savagely. "Get him a chit for a flight outfit and leave the rest to me."

So it was settled, and when they went into the bar Mac introduced Barney to the others in his flight: Jerry Parkington, his deputy flight leader; Ollie Bates, who did tricks with beer glasses; Hugh Simons and Boppo Sprague, the Mutt and Jeff of the outfit. They all looked at Barney as if he were fresh out of an asylum.

"I thought Mac was a friend of yours," Parkington said under his breath when he heard what the correspondent had bought. "You know that T-33 is practically a trainer job. No guns or anything."

Corinth nodded, but he didn't look too certain. "It might turn out to be a milk run," he said hopefully.

"There are no milk runs where Mac is concerned. That guy can make a routine engine test as hot as a dogfight. He's still the same old Mac; a great pilot, but still trying to win the war on his own."

"Still—I guess I ought to go—once."

"I hope you're in shape. Ever ride in any high-speed equipment? Have you any idea what it's like to pull out of a 600-mph dive?"

Barney avoided Parkington's eyes. "I think I'm all right—that way. There's nothing wrong with me except . . ." And he tried to explain why he had never been able to get into the armed services.

A puzzled frown delayed Parkington's response. He put down his mug of beer. "I can't imagine anything like that. It doesn't show, but it must affect your outlook."

"It's just something you don't talk about." Barney tried to smile. "No one can really understand it, and I'm not sure what I'm trying to explain."

Parkington replied vaguely, "Of course. How can you explain not enjoying something you've never experienced?"

"Well, it hasn't affected me so far, and I guess Mac will make it as easy as he can."

"He'll give you plenty of opportunity to see everything. I know that MacLean." Park was living only to get Mac's lead position in the formation. He'd had all he wanted of Captain MacLean. The whole flight admired him, but their admiration wasn't the kind that is nurtured in Sunday school.

They were briefed on Mission 71 at 04:50 hours. The room was dank and musty and its features stood out stark and harsh under the brittle glare of unshielded bulbs. The pilots drifted in, sleepy and blinking, gorged with a tasteless breakfast.

The strike was outlined on the wall map with lengths of scarlet worsted, blue grease pencil, and bleary crosshatching.

The Old Man was saying, "Formation will be important on this mission. Your main target will be the advanced tank-repair depot here at P'yŏngyang. At the approximate Time over Target the B-29's will be attacking the Wosan ammunition dump and the Aussies will fly a Mustang sweep over Chinnamp'o, mainly to draw enemy fighters from this area."

"This'll be good," Mac whispered to Barney. "You'll maybe see the smoke from that bomber attack, too."

Corinth said nothing. He was chilled, and the breakfast was pumping a rancid tang back into his throat.

The S-2 officer snapped off the lights and threw a photograph of the target area on a screen. "The repair depot is square, approximately twenty-two hundred feet on each side," he explained with a length of picture molding for a pointer. "Your approach will be here. Your aiming point here. . . ."

"You're gonner get a story, buster," MacLean added. "We'll go down with each ship of our flight. We'll make four passes instead of one—see?"

"You'll go all the way down, even though you carry no bombs?" Corinth inquired.

"I'm taking rockets. Had a launching rack fixed on during the night. We'll give 'em hell!"

The weather officer crawled up on the platform. He waited

until a vertical cross section of the weather over Korea was flashed on. "It's not good—but it's not too bad. On take-off you'll have six tenths, thin cirro-stratus above twenty-five thousand. Visibility two to three miles in haze. Thin patches of alto-stratus up here at twelve thousand with tops at fourteen thousand. You won't have to worry about freezing your tails off." He closed with the standard jet-fighter gag.

He got his laugh—crockery-brittle—but it was choked off by the opening roar of an F-80 jet engine screaming from a nearby dispersal point.

Corinth was fixed up with a heated liner, a fleece-lined leather suit, and a Mae West. The supply sergeant checked his parachute and told him to bring it back if it didn't work. Helmet, goggles, and oxygen mask were bundled into his arms and he followed Mac out to the weapons carrier with the buoyancy of a condemned man. A Red Cross girl in the corridor offered him a cup of coffee, but Barney never saw her. Three jet pilots were on their knees before an unshaven padre who was chanting a toneless prayer.

Once the dank pall of the briefing room was shrugged off, the pilots worked up a counterfeit program of horseplay. They straddled the hoods of jeeps, dangled their long legs over the tailboards of the trucks, and bellowed libelous invectives as they circled the perimeter track. Corinth huddled down and wondered how much of that he could write.

"Climb down!" Mac ordered as the carrier dragged to a halt before a banked-up dispersal bay. The line crew was stretched out on work tarpaulins beneath the needle nose of the two-seater jet.

"Where's your regular ship?" Corinth asked, for something to say.

"Over in the next bay. The one with *Lady Guinevere* painted on the nose. Get it? *Lady Guinevere.* You were dancing with her a few nights ago." Mac scowled.

Corinth dropped most of his loose gear in the dust. Then he said. "Lady Guinevere? Oh, I see. That's for Gwyn."

"Yeh, Gwyn. The gal you can't remember much about."

"Gwyn would like that," Corinth replied, and wondered who thought it up. It didn't sound like Mac.

He tried to remember more about Gwyn. He had danced with a girl who was custom built and moved like a thoroughbred. Things like that he could remember. Her nonchalance was bewitching—and misleading, for her pride was in one man, and Corinth knew there would never be any other in her life. He was, as Parkington had said, a great pilot. The kind who fought wars with savage intensity; just as he lived every other phase of his life. Barney wondered what Gwyn would think of her man if he ever got back.

"I like the name." And Corinth looked across at the script lettering again.

That only whipped the turmoil in MacLean's mind and put the red ball of hate on the wheel: sure he likes the name, but five will get you ten Gwyn doesn't mention that country-club business. The Red Cross meeting, maybe her mother's asthma, and all the clinical details; but there won't be a line about Creepy-Corinth.

In the next few minutes Mac made sure Barney's helmet was fitted correctly and that his oxygen line was in order. He stood on the wing and carefully strapped the correspondent into the front seat.

"Look, Barney," he explained petulantly. "You're in a jet and she can do six hundred—downhill. If we get into trouble—well, first I'll release the canopy. You loosen your seat straps and wait until I tilt her over so you can clear safely. You know about the chute?"

"You mean—jump out? I thought we went out automatically. Ejector-seat business."

"That's comic-book stuff. You get out yourself, if you have

to," Mac stated bluntly, "but don't go until I signal—and don't foul the stick."

Mac plugged in his phones so he could listen in on their radio contacts and then slipped into the control seat behind. The line crew stood off and stared up at Corinth while Mac kicked in the starter and opened up the jet engine. At first there was a choked roar and the T-33 vibrated like a panting rhino, but gradually the pressure power smoothed off and much of the initial roar was filtered out. Barney heard Mac talking to Parkington.

"You lead the formation, Park. We'll take the tail spot."

"Oh, Mac!" Parkington protested. "You got a passenger. Give him a break."

"I'm giving him a break. He can only see forward from his seat, and he wants to see what it's like. You take the lead, Park."

"You're the doctor," Parkington answered, and Mac rolled his jet out of the dispersal bay.

One by one the F-80's raced down the long runway, each leaving a farewell belch of kerosene stench and blue smoke. As MacLean hoiked his ship off the runway, Barney sat huddled against the back of his seat with his fists clenched across his middle. He felt as though he were locked inside a rampaging torpedo.

Within minutes they were high in the sky and Japan was far behind. Corinth had relaxed somewhat by now and was able to concentrate on the four jets ahead and below. They seemed to be fitted together loosely, like the self-same parts of a jigsaw puzzle dropped on a tattletale-gray tablecloth. All the confusion of the take-off had been eradicated and Barney sensed an indescribable rushing sensation; there was no vibration at all—just a quiet tenseness that kept the hair on his neck tingling.

"Too bad you didn't bring a camera," Mac said into his helmet. Barney tried to turn around and look at his pilot, but it seemed impossible to twist his neck. "However," Mac went on, "you probably couldn't handle it if we got to kicking around any. The pressure gets rough unless you're in shape."

"There's nothing like that—wrong with me," Barney protested. "I'll be all right, no matter what happens. I'm usually lucky, Mac."

"Sure," Mac said to himself, "you'd probably like something to happen. You'd like a story to crow about; to write how you went on a hot mission to get a feature—but the jet you flew in, piloted by a home-town pal, got knocked down. Wouldn't you like to make that sort of headline! The intrepid war correspondent might even figure how he could escape and get back through the lines by swiping a Red tank. You'd think of something hot."

Aloud Mac said, "You'd better be lucky."

They began to slice wings through the fringe of piled-up clouds and Barney wondered whether they were over Korea. Frost brushed powdered designs on the canopy until Mac turned up the heaters and Barney saw the four jets below had huddled into an even tighter pattern, and a new babble of voices filled his helmet as he again tried to look back at Mac for reassurance. The pilot was listening intently, his eyes slitted, as he unscrambled the word signals.

"There's an L-5 below somewhere, spotting targets for some other outfit. We can expect hate any minute now."

"Are we over Korea?"

"Sure. We're north of Seoul. We should be over the target any minute now. Keep your eyes open."

"How should I know?" Barney protested, and then something exploded above them. He cringed and heard Mac laugh. He wondered what the explosion was. He looked ahead, but all four jets were still in that cramped formation, and then the pressure came on suddenly as Mac tilted their nose down and plunged through the cloud carpet.

They came out over a drab patchwork of rice paddies, snag-toothed hills, and a few roads that seemed to come from nowhere and have no destination. Now he was looking down the tails of the jets and seeing the stern points of the wing tanks, the long, slim penetration bombs just outside the air scoops and the quartet of pencil-like rockets under the wings. They seemed puny weapons to attack a factory or a concentration of tanks— no more offensive than the feathered darts he had tossed in the locker room of the club back home only five nights before.

Mac bellowed again. "Keep your eyes open. We're going down. Watch Parkington. He'll go in first with his rockets and then come back with his heavy stuff."

Corinth's eyes were open—wide open—as if they were being pulled apart so a doctor could flick out a cinder. He worked his cheeks in an attempt to get the lids back and stop the tears. He was trapped in some compression chamber and all the ooze in his joints was being squeezed out.

"There goes Parkington!"

Corinth looked, but there was no jet in sight. Finally he saw one alongside of them—Parkington was going down almost vertical, and they were winging down with him! Barney peered over the nose and saw the saw-edged design of a set of roofs blasting up, widening and enlarging at a preposterous rate. Two smoky streams swept from the jet alongside them and mushroomed into a maze of gray-blue metal. There was a puny explosion, and it seemed to Corinth that he was looking at a badly focused strip of newsreel film snapped from a plunging bomber. Because of the pressure, he saw nothing else until they were back winging along with another jet job.

"See that?" Mac shouted over the intercom. "You see Park's crackers nose in there? One of them, anyway."

Corinth saw nothing like that; he was trying to focus his eyes on the frame of the windscreen.

"Boppo's going down now. Keep your eyes open. That Boppo's good!"

They were tail up again, rushing at the tilted world, and Barney attempted to brace himself, but his feet and legs were solid marble, so he forced his head back against a metal plate

behind him and listened to the frantic intercourse filling his
helmet. He saw Boppo start down, and Boppo's rockets splutter
away—and that was the last he saw of Boppo.

Mac was screaming like a madman as they yanked out of the
chest-crushing dive and came up through a column of smoke.
Mac choked out: "Boppo augered in! Boppo didn't pull out!"

Corinth let the war go its way. He was helpless against the
punishment of pressure. He retched at the stench of his own
sweat and wondered what they were complaining about back
home—that jets couldn't stay over the target more than fifteen
minutes. Fifteen minutes? They had been diving and zooming
amid this carnage for hours. Dive—scream—lurch—zoom—peel
off. . . . Dive—scream . . . Boppo had been dead so long they could
have built a memorial in his honor.

Barney was exhausted, spent, physically flayed, and mentally
groggy. He wondered why Mac continued these repeated passes
when he could have stayed above the target, circling it in com-
parative safety. What more was there to see that could be put
into words? This hideous flash from a molten world. A picture
spewing from invisible rolls, toned with the gray-white of his
everyday world, but capable of wounding the mind, leaving
scar tissue of memory that would never fully heal.

Rockets had spurted from outboard racks; bombs had plunged
in a wide arc toward the tangled wreckage below, and a man
had been devoured in the fiery maw of the writhing dragon.
It all boiled into a pattern of war and Barney hated his puny
part in it and willingly would have traded Boppo's merciful
plunge into oblivion, could he forget what he had seen—to be
excused from ever typing the words on paper and thus adding
pages to a scarlet history.

But as the frantic babble of battle went on about his ears, he
worked out a lead paragraph, and sifted his mental reactions and
splintered impressions amid the frenzy of fighting, the spatter of

coordinates, the patois of a service, the profane boasts of accomplishment.

"I went on a jet-fighter strike today with a formation attacking a tank-repair depot in North Korea," he repeated in his mind through the sound-track distraction whipping through his earphones. "I have seen war as it has never been seen before...."

MacLean was bellowing: "You've been fool-lucky in the past. I hope you're lucky now."

The implication made Corinth stiffen, and he managed to get his head around and look at the pilot who was an enraged beast glaring with lynx eyes at the dials and switches banked before him. Corinth looked past him and realized they were back in formation, skimming the jagged ridges of the Korean hills.

"I'm always lucky," he responded. "When do I turn on the influence?"

"We got trouble. We were clipped when we took down our rockets." Barney wondered when all that took place.

"See those red lights on that panel?" Mac snarled. "They mean trouble. The radio is out—I can't contact the other guys—except by signal flare." He continued some frantic business with the switches. "Our main tank has been opened up."

The lights on the panel made no sense to Corinth. "You mean we force-land somewhere in South Korea?"

Mac wagged his head negatively. "We need six thousand feet—even if we get far enough south. They're bulldozing a strip somewhere, but it's not ready yet."

"Don't these tanks self-seal?" Barney peered back at the other jets.

"Only in the company catalogues. I'll try to figure something. You'll know what to expect when you see what colored flare I pop off."

Barney wondered why a self-sealing tank wouldn't seal. He turned back, hunched up, and worked out another lead for his story. "I went on a jet-fighter strike today with Captain Robert

MacLean. We were hit over the target and had to force-land in enemy territory . . ."

Then he remembered that they had indeed been hit and that a tank was so damaged it no longer held fuel—fuel they needed to get back to safety.

"How bad is it, Mac?" he finally asked over the intercom.

The pilot took another look and the cursor of his skill flipped along the slide rule of his mind, and the product left him numb. The bitterness and cold hate for the man up front who had unwittingly set up this predicament came back to intensify the percentage against them.

"Watch this—you'll know." Mac reached down for his signal pistol, inserted a cartridge, and rolled back the canopy a few inches. The spluttering fire ball leaped out, arched forward, and eventually died against a patch of azure-blue sky. "There's your story, chum," he said bitterly.

The correspondent stared at the faint smoke streaks drifting down the sky and then turned and looked at Mac, with resignation in his eyes. "I don't get it, Mac. The flare, I mean."

"You saw it, didn't you? You saw that red flare. You know what that means, don't you?"

"Red? . . . I can't tell what color it was, Mac. I saw it, but I'm color blind, Mac. Everything's—like a dull gray to me."

Mac closed the canopy and stared unbelievingly—just as Parkington had. "You can't tell colors, Barney? Color blind. Is that it? You can't see those red lights on the fuel panel? You didn't know what color the flare was?"

Barney hoped they'd at least get down in South Korea where he could file his story. He had all the details racked away now. A straight narrative story of what it's like to do a rocket raid with the jets. What it feels like to go in at six hundred mph, and what you see when penetration bombs bite in. He had a sweet line about Boppo Sprague who represented all men who had fought and died. He knew that line would please a lot of people who probably hadn't smiled in weeks. That Boppo was a great little guy.

MacLean stared at the fuel gauge again and came up with a great resolution. "He can't tell colors—red, blues, or greens. He can't see the colors of the trees, the flowers, or blue sky. Everything's gray in his life—no colors in his world. He can't see a woman's hair, her lips, or her eyes. He doesn't know what a real woman looks like. He danced with Gwyn, but doesn't know she has copper-colored hair, that her eyes are periwinkle blue, or the shade of lipstick she uses. He can't tell whether she's wearing a Nile-green dress or yellow sweater—and what those colors do for her. To him, Gwyn's just a figure in a lousy fogged-out snapshot."

Mac went to work manipulating the pet cocks and pumps that would transfer fuel from the ruptured tank, pumping it into the wing tanks, checking the flow, and weighing the net against the mileage back to safety. It was a task that had to be done right, or disaster would take over. A man had to know and remember the sequence of fuel flow, the pressures, and the devious paths the precious liquid could safely take to be salvaged and stored in an undamaged container. It was no time for trial and error. One mistake in by-passing, and the priceless gallons would be lost—the few gallons that meant all the difference between a ghastly pile-up in enemy territory or a belly landing on what the bulldozer boys had already hacked out near Taegu.

He slapped Barney across the shoulders and grinned. "Don't worry, pal. I'll get you back somewhere. You'll get your story, keed!"

It took more than fighting to sit and work it out. It took pilotage of the finest order, a skill and degree of physical discipline not even Barney Corinth would ever understand, interpret, or put into words. It took fortitude, staying power, and the determination to accept no compromise; but there are no words for the explanation of such courage.

"This'll be a beaut, Barney," Mac went on as he sat through those fear-sickened minutes checking the responses on the various dials. "Like you said, you'll be able to tell Gwyn what it was like. I'd never be able to tell her. When I'm with her, all I can do is sit and look at her—just speechless."

All this time the T-33 was maintaining her position in the formation, roaring like a winged comet through the broken pattern of cloud, protruding peaks, and the opposition of turbulence and updrafts. It took a pilot such as Captain MacLean to salvage the last few pints of power-producing solution from that shell-damaged system and store it in what secure space he had left.

It took all that, and a guy like Barney Corinth to tell it—after they had belly landed on the strip at Taegu.